The beginning

It was a bright sunny day in the city of Skylark, the birds sang as they flew above the small pink flowered trees. Green grass covered every lawn that protected the mansion-like houses, and kids were just ending their summer vacation as Fall knocked on the door to relieve Summer from its duties.

Paul, a short kid with faded black hair and brown eyes, sat on his bed. He began to stare at the wall that harbored him inside of a crooked home. There wasn't much to do because whether he committed a crime or not, there was never a time he wasn't in trouble

Lucyfer, an above average sized woman, shoved her upper body into his room with irritation on her face.

"Is your room cleaned?" she asked with a thick African American accent.

"Yes," he responded with slight annoyance.

"Excuse me, it's yes ma'am. I'm not your friend, I'm your parent," she scolded.

"I wish I was with my *real* parents," he mumbled.

"What?" her voice grew angrier. "You know if your brother were here then I wouldn't be getting such smartass answers from you," she snarled, leaving the room and walking down the hall to the other room where other kids slept.

Lucyfer is a woman who fosters kids for income. Retired from the state of Skylark she spent most of her days watching television, eating food, buying clothes, or going to church every Sunday. Paul was adopted by this woman when he was just eight. Along with his brother, who was adopted at the age of eleven, they walked to the bus together but never went to the same school. They rode on the same bus, but never entered the same school doors.

In frustration and realization, Sean began to rebel against her evil ways of raising. Lucyfer responded by throwing him outside in the cold, making him walk from school if he had any after school activities. She threatened him with knives and her younger male child. He was a man where if you fought back, there would probably be no surviving. As a child that grew up with his parents both vocally and physically fighting, Sean was naturally scared.

It got to the point where his life was on the line multiple times in this home. Frustrated, his brother reached out to the police for help but when the accusations were presented to Lucyfer, she made Paul lie for her. This angered Sean, shunning Paul permanently. It was around the age of fourteen for Paul and seventeen for Sean when Sean threatened her home and was permanently removed. Distraught at the fact that he had to face high school alone, Paul was scared of the real world.

Bored, Paul didn't know what to do. His room was clean, the basement was dirty as rolls of misplaced carpet scattered the floor, the insulation was torn apart by the dogs that were kept from the foster agency she slipped through. In a small section of the basement, couches sat around a coffee table like teenagers around a campfire. A fifty inch box television supervised the carpet that laid underneath, all done by Paul. Going outside wasn't something Paul enjoyed doing, he had no friends since Lucyfer kept him in solitude for most of the time. There was too much to worry about, such as being a second parent to the kids, cooking, cleaning, washing clothes, etc. He loved to study martial arts, however, Lucyfer never allowed violence. With no privacy, his computer and room were often searched.

The only solitude Paul could confide in was the book he was writing, it was about a man who traveled space and the multiverses to protect those who were in need. For those who have nobody else they can call upon for help, a man everyone could hide behind when the main hero cannot win, his name was Bison. He was the shining light next to his brother Bull, Byron, and a guardian, they cannot be stopped. He furiously typed away his emotions, getting lost with every word as the feeling of joy he's lost flourished through his mind. He also kept another book, a journal of which he kept his most personal secrets. He clicked away from his book, opening a new tab to his journal.

"It's been a hard day," he wrote in his journal. "I have school to worry about and Lucyfer would kill me if I start failing. I don't like school but it's the only place I have people I can call friends. The place I live is about a thirty minute walk from the nearest gas station, so even if I wanted to hangout with friends it would still be a journey to get to places. Work has been made easy, though the threat of walking to and from lingers in the tension built from the hot and cold days. Lucyfer seems psychotic, but it also seems as if she cares, in her own way. This is why I haven't tried to run like my brother Sean. You can do certain things to be on her good side, but you have to be careful because one slip-up could lead to being punished. It's already bad enough I'm stuck here with kids moving in and out, like it's some kind of babysitting business.

It sickens me to know that people are like her, harboring children then lying and tricking whenever she has been exposed. Her greed pisses me off the more I see it, to the point where it disgusts me. Every smile she got every time she saw a cute dress or a cute purse, I knew deep down she didn't need it and that the mortgage needed to be paid. Life would be better if I could leave, but I cannot disobey the one who raised me and took me in, right? Who knows who my parents are, but was it all a lie to be turned into an image you didn't desire. So when things go awry, it's better to write them off and send them away? Just like my brother, he didn't go with the flow and he had to be removed. She called him crazy and they believed her because I lied because I was afraid of what would happen if I had said something. Would they have left me there for a night, and if they did, what would she do to me?

The pain he went through because of me is all of my fault, and now he hates me for it. The last time we talked there was nothing but hatred in his tone, as if I were a bad memory. I hate the way people look at the house like we have it good when mentally we are failing. Oh journal my journal, will you keep my secrets?

-Paul"

Chapter 2

Early Mornings

Paul's bedroom lit up, showing the bed that was across from his bed and a dresser in front as he sat up in his bed, rubbing his eyes as he realized that today was his first day back in school.

"Time to get up," Lucyfer taunted as she turned her back to his opened door. "Get your clothes and shoes on, you'll eat breakfast at school."

The morning was warm and the sun was still hidden due to daylight savings. It was August, Paul loved these mornings mainly because of the warmth he felt from the humidity that still lingered in the air. He often enjoyed spending time outside of the house, going to school to hangout with friends and make jokes. He basically did anything he wasn't allowed to do at home at school, to an extent.

As he rubbed the sleep from his eyes, his vision was still a little blurry as he turned his attention towards the cage next to the dresser. The guinea pig that sat in the corner of his room squeaked loudly, indicating it wanted either food or water.

He stood up from his bed and walked over to the small closet just behind the door leading into his room, to the left. Paul opened his closet, looking around he saw a lot of expensive clothes hanging up and some junk on the floor where his guinea pigs' food was.

"I hate wearing expensive clothes." he thought to himself as he yanked a yellow shirt with a horse on it from its hanger. "I can never wear T-shirts or anything fun. I hate my life," he complained as he picked up the guinea pig food and draped his shirt over his shoulder.

Turning around with the food in one hand and his shirt on his shoulder, he walked over to his guinea pigs cage and opened it, exposing the fat brown fluffball. He reached inside and grabbed his food container, submerging it into the food bag then out again. He placed the now full food bowl onto the clean wood bedding and began to pet Richard. He thought to name his guinea pig after a pink rabbit in his favorite cartoon when he saw how much he loved to eat.

"Are you thirsty?" Paul asked as he observed the empty bottle attached to the side of the cage.

He unhooked the metal bottle from the cage and let the bottle drop into his hand. Standing up, Paul walked out of his room to the room immediately to his right. He flicked on the lights, exposing a windowless bathroom with white dual sinks and a shower head that looked over the stained tub. He walked over to the sink on the right, remembering the warning to not touch the sink on the left.

He unscrewed the bottle and lifted the hole to the spout of the sink as the water neatly fell together in a straight line. He filled the bottle up, dumping it out over and over again to clean away any bacteria before filling it to the brim. He screwed the mouthpiece back onto the bottle. Leaving the bathroom, he turned off the lights and walked back into his room. He walked up to his guinea pigs cage and attached the water bottle, letting the water slowly drip onto the wood bedding. He closed the door and grabbed the all black ankle shoes placed to the left of the dresser,

It wasn't often Paul got a room to himself, he usually shared it with another foster kid or his brother. He didn't mind the isolation, the silence let him think as freely as he wanted. Without a lot of friends and little support from others about his situation, he preferred to be alone. There were two kids in the room down the hallway next to the bathroom. They woke up later since they were under the age of ten.

Walking out of his room prepared for the day, Lucyfer met him atop of the steps to escort him to the garage door. Paul didn't eat breakfast at home since the school provided two meals. He walked down the fifteen stairs, counting every step as he descended into the foyer. There was a silence that carried with them into the washroom that held both the old washer and dryer meant to break down, to grab his green one strapped bag. He walked out to the garage, since Sean kicked the front door down, passing a tan SUV before reaching the big metal door.

He reached down to the bar and gripped it with little effort as he heaved the light door above his head. He left the mouth of the garage wide open as he walked out onto the black driveway, turning around and shutting the garage before he continued his journey.

"If only you didn't leave," Paul thought as he turned around to see the half a mansion house tower over him. "This could have all been avoided, maybe."

He enjoyed thinking, it was the only way he could express himself truly. Usually loud in certain classes, Paul didn't feel like being the hype man today. It was more of a relaxing quiet day. He thought of everything, ranging from school work to his book.

"I hope Lucyfer doesn't find out about the vase I broke yesterday, I hid it in the basement. Knowing my luck she's going to go downstairs and find whatever to get pissed about. If anything, she should be sitting on the couch until I get home to hand her the remote that's an arm stretch away. Now, onto Bison, what if…" his thoughts were interrupted as he arrived at the bus stop, the sound of teenagers was heard as he approached the group.

He had neighborhood friends but he never got the chance to really hangout. Jake was a tall, slim, and blonde-haired kid, not much younger than Paul. He very much enjoyed his company, probably because he was close to his best friend Chris. Nigel was taller and more slim than Jake, only his face was a lot flatter. He hardly ever saw Nigel around school, only afterwards when he didn't have practice for basketball or before school at the bus stop. Jason was as tall as Nigel but wore glasses. He was a class clown and got a lot of popular kids' attention. He was someone Paul liked being around when he felt like being rowdy. To him they were annoying, being around them made him feel small since he was never allowed to do the things they were. Drinking, driving, smoking, anything teenagers aren't allowed to do.

"Gosh," he thought as he stood there in his black sweat pants and a blank red T-shirt. "I don't like school but I hate it at home, everything that happens is typically blamed on me. If only I could protect those I don't know who are in the same situation I am, maybe not in a reality such as this one. Martial arts is fun, but it's useless in terms of defense only in my reality, nobody attacks me. I think that Bison should protect people, no matter who they are. Whether it be man, child, or woman. Or maybe he should just go throughout the universes to protect them from the evil that's trying to conquer the solar systems within said universes. Seems like if he could travel from one universe to another, he could automatically be in another onmi-verse, hmmm."

His thoughts were interrupted yet again by a long yellow bus approaching to take them to school. He climbed up the stairs, being the last one on the bus. He sat in the back since he liked to listen to his music. It was safe to pull out his phone now since Lucyfer was nowhere nearby. Paul often enjoyed listening to heavy metal, dubstep, or anything that relates to dark thoughts that helps remind him of better days which fuels his inner rage. He sat there staring out of the window at the trees zipping by, followed by houses every now and then.

Chapter 3

The Skylark School

Kids were not very excited about going to school due to its size. **The Skylark Everything School was the only school in this town, the mayor thought it would be a bad idea since he didn't** want to overpopulate the school. He came up with a solution, however, to ensure kids had their education separated between groups of grades. It took up almost the entire town, there was nowhere to turn without running into its walls. Preschoolers and kindergarteners were on the first floor, ranging from about fifty football fields. The first through third graders were on the second level, fourth through sixth graders were on the third level, seventh to the ninth graders were on the fourth floor. The rest, tenth to twelfth, were on the fifth floor.

"Strange," Paul thought as he approached the twelve stone steps that lead up to the small dual doors in comparison. "It would be more fitting to have more schools for the separate grades, but I guess being the second island in the world can do things like this. Weird about that too," he pondered as he approached the doors and grasped the thick handle. Pulling at the door, he realized that the door was heavier than normal.

Someone from behind put a hand on Paul's shoulder, causing him to jump a bit. He turned around to be confronted by a short chubby kid with dirty blonde hair, Chris.

"Hey Paul, how was Summer? I bet you got all the chicks." he teased as his two friends approached them.

"Not really, I worked the entire time and it was awesome," he bragged as he stared at the ground, hoping to get more alone time before the school bell began.

One by one, they walked into the school as more and more students shoved their way inside. The chatter in the air could be heard from miles away as buses emptied their load of kids onto the school grounds.

Paul noticed a stack of papers sitting on a desk in front of a singular pillar, it was a layout of the school in words and it read as followed:

"Welcome to the Skylark Everything School, where every need is supplied. The hallways are large enough to fit two lines of students, one traveling in one direction while the other travels the opposite. There are numbers on black plates next to the doors indicating their relationship. The lockers are slim and a lock is already pre-installed. When you enter the school, there are no doors but a narrow hallway with a singular pillar and desk that leads to a small opening. In that opening you will find three doors, the one on the left leads to the kindergarten classrooms while the one on the right leads to the Preschool classrooms. The door straight ahead leads into the cafeteria, which if kept straight, will lead you to another opening with three doors. One with double doors straight ahead, which leads to the Guidance Corner. This room is huge, the secretary sits in front of a huge wall with an opening on each side. There, you can state your issue, but we do take action. The left side will lead you to the guidance counselors office, while the right will guide you to the principal's office.

"The door on the right will direct you to the stairs where you can access any part of the student body classes, ranging from first to third grade on the second floor. The third floor will take you to the fourth through sixth grade floors, seventh through ninth will be located on the fourth floor. The rest will be on the fifth floor, while above that are college classes. Nobody but authorized students are allowed on these floors. If seen, immediate action will be taken..

"The door on the left will lead you to another opening with two doors on each side. The door on the left will lead to the gymnasium, which leads to a backyard with twenty acres of space. Every level has a gymnasium that leads to a yard, however the yards on these floors sit on concrete. The dirt and sun are natural, though the sun cannot shine in but through the windows. Surrounding this beautiful piece of land is a fence so that no student may leave the premises. There are playgrounds and equipment for the younger ages to use.

"The door on the right leads to the auditorium with fifty-million seats, this is by far the largest room in the school. With a projector the size of a monument displayed on the wall of a humongous stage. Awards are given out here, along with special meetings," it wrote.

Paul entered the small opening and entered through the door straight ahead. They passed the tables and students that occupied them, he always ignored certain students. Everyone knew the name of Paul, but it was rare anyone talked to him.

"Do you know where any of the classes are? I've always been confused," Chris asked as they walked through the door that lead to the larger opening.

They entered the door on the right that led to the stairs, making a single file line as they climbed towards the fifth floor.

Paul, who was first in line, replied.

"Well, the entire school is split based on simplicity, so I think they divide grades into subjects depending on the placement of the school," he explained as he stared at the ceiling.

"What?" Chris asked at a loss for words.

"Basically the front of the school is science, and it may be like that on every floor to the corresponding grade. I wonder if there are any bathrooms near?" Paul asked as they passed the first door in the stairwell, climbing to the second level.

"Yeah, but speaking of which, we're on floor 2 and I got to pee," Chris mentioned as he trailed off, pulling at the exit from the stairs.

"You'd think they'd put a bathroom on the bottom floors, but they are in the actual classroom," Paul began to think as he watched the door close. "Wait," he thought as he realized the danger of Chris's decision.

He grabbed the tall door handle and whipped the door open, almost tearing it from the hinges as the sound of the door smacking against the wall echoed. He stared down a very narrow hallway as his body began to go limp and his head was lighter than a feather.

Suddenly, the hallway stretched, the disfiguration made him dizzy as stumbled around. His thoughts began to race as he dragged himself against the lockers, trying to keep what little balance he had left.

"How the hell do you disappear after closing a door?" He thought to himself as he began to regain control of both his mind and body.

There were poster boards of children's artwork as he passed the dark classrooms yet, Chris was nowhere to be found, and the smell grew more and more potent the further back he walked. Some pictures were cute while others were of the darker variety. There was one that caught Paul's attention.

"Weird," he thought. "This one looks like a principal beating a kid, and the others watching. What the hell?" There seemed to be quite a few similar to this, however they all read "NIGHTMARE" underneath.

"Is this some kind of excuse to write it off, like it wasn't real? Seems like these kids wouldn't lie about something so big, why would they?" Paul thought as he inspected more and more pictures. "The bigger question is, what's the truth behind this school. From the shady building structure to the principle within, something isn't entirely piecing together. For a principle, he was nowhere to be seen on the first say, so how is he controlling this huge school? You'd think there would be multiple principles, but the letter never mentioned any other principles." he pondered as he began to make his way down the hall.

He felt uncomfortable the deeper and deeper he got as the hairs on his body were beginning to stand. The hallway was dimmed due to the kids being absent, yet there were no windows or exits that lead to another section of the school. It was just one long hallway with classroom doors, yet every door was locked and dark. The hallway seemed to stretch on forever as Paul inspected the old decorations hanging across the width of the hall.

"Shit, this is by far the creepiest hallway I've seen. Not to mention, there aren't any children here. Since it's early, they won't be here until later, right? I'm still left to wonder, where are all the teachers?" He asked himself as he looked for Chris, hopefully to get away from this hallway.

A hand appeared out of a dark room, gripping Paul's arm, yanking him in. Before he had the time to scream, a palm was put against his mouth to silence him.

"Shhh, you're not allowed in this hallway," he whispered as a warning, lowering his hand. His voice was deep, raspy, and he smelled like old tires and gunk from a sewer. "They'll punish you," he harshly whispered.

Letting him go, Paul turned around to see the man's dirty face not too high above his own height. His beard was unkempt and shaggy, along with his hair. He stood at approximately six feet, and his eyes were wide with a soft face.

"What's going on?" Paul asked as the fear he felt washed away as if something unnatural calmed him.

Paul thought that he would rather get answers from him since it seemed as if this man was trying to help.

"Listen, there's not much explaining to do, nor do we have the time. The principal put in charge of this school is corrupt and is apparently using this school to cover himself as a regular human. In reality, he's a demon from the omniverse parallel to us. Running away from those authorities, he retreated to this universe to hide from the Priestess.

"Any man, woman, or child that disobeyed him would be severely punished and yet nobody knew his motive. Be warned, an invasion is coming, " the man explained.

"What?" Paul pondered, confused at the words he was hearing.

"He found out about me and threatened to take the planet along with the surrounding universes and any multiverse it leads into, leading to the death of this omniverse."

Pauls' mind began to race, he didn't know what to think. "If the principle were to be evil, wouldn't he have just killed the entire student body already, and why hide in this universe then destroy it when you've been found out? Couldn't he just kill the man who knows his true identity and spare us." He began to think of solutions as if there were a way out. "Why're you telling me this anyway?" Paul asked calmly.

"There's a deity I used to work for, he's known to watch over the omni-verses. It's been a century and some years, but he had me in the position to protect anything that threatened the end of an omniverse. Listen," the man commanded as he started to walk off into the dark. "There is nowhere safe," his voice began to fade into the dark when a light suddenly turned on, revealing quite a normal sized room. "But in this room we are, it's a room I built myself. Being completely invisible to the naked eye, it makes for great privacy." His eyes began to stare at Pauls' foot, making him feel uncomfortable.

Out of instinct he looked down to see what he was looking at, and to his surprise there was a string tied to his ankle. It stretched to the door, leading into the hallway.

"Seems like it's already started, the crew you're meant to be apart of is already being put in play."

"What're you talking about, a crew? Does this mean that my book," Paul began to pace around the room as his mind raced, looking at the empty bookshelves. "So you're telling me you're only here to keep us alive, but there's a reason you're stepping down?"

"That's almost correct, but you won't be the one appointed. Let's just say that your future starts now, young one. How old are you anyway?"

"Sixteen," he replied.

"Ah," he ignored, picking up a picture on his desk. "When we started we were only a year younger. Sadly the fate of that omniverse hung in the balance on a mission we were supposed to complete. The highest bargaining chip was our only option, yet it did not save us all. I was told to go out and get reinforcements when in reality, it was just a way to send me away and live to tell the story. I wandered endless years searching for them and to no end, I could never find them. Until one day I got captured by the High Priest of Evil, instead of watching over to protect, he watches over to destroy," he began to explain again as he put the picture down. He sat on the empty desk, crossing his legs and folding his hands.

"There's been a war between the two since the creation of existence. For endless eras, warriors have died, soldiers were sacrificed, and in the end to no progress but a standstill. There are no other mythical Gods or goddesses that dare to challenge the two, and since they can give and take away immortality with just the snap of a finger, they don't bother to try. If the two beings fought, it would mean the end of existence, or a fate worse than that. A fate where existence would never exist again."

Paul stood there, processing the information he had just acquired as he stared at the red string tied around his ankle.

"Is this janitor crazy?" he thought, leaning against the wall behind him with a thumb hovering over his lip. "If I do believe him, it could mean adventures, but we'll also be facing supercilious people."

"Oh yeah," he exclaimed, interrupting his thought. "You'll be facing immortals who get bored and decide to kill a bunch of things. Well, not all of them. Some are men that have been outcasted from society, or men that've been constantly beaten in battle. At the same time, there are many reasons to want to destroy the omniverses. The main reason me and my crew defended omni-verses was because the omni-watcher of said omni-verse was under attack. Unfortunately, my allies were killed in a battle and my time is about to run short. He will fill you in on the rest but you have to leave," he taught as he stood from his desk.

He rushed over to Paul, standing in front of him as if to signal that he'd lead the way.

"Wait, I have so many questions," Paul pleaded as the janitor shoved him towards the door.

"If you're as smart as they say you'll listen to my advice and enact on it. You've already got the tools, you just need your allies."

Being pushed out of the door, Paul tripped on his feet as he turned around and saw that the door had vanished. All that could be seen was the wall, and from beyond the wall he heard the janitor speak,

"Oh and also, most of the kids here are just spirits, they've been killed by the principle. Maybe your one friend is a spirit too, be careful because they will attack."

Chapter 4

Paul's Curse

Silence fell as the lights in the hall began to flicker violently as Paul looked down at the string tied to his ankle. He looked up to see his friend, Chris, suddenly standing face to face with Paul to greet him with a creepy ear to ear wide smile.

"Hey buddy," he verbalized in an awkward cheerful voice. "How's it going?"

As every student suddenly appeared out of nowhere, they began to rush him from behind.

"Damnit," he thought as he quickly looked behind himself then in front.

They touched him and began to yank at his arms and legs until they eventually tossed him further down the hallway. He sat up and kneeled to a crouch, ready for a battle he wasn't prepared for. Realizing he was surrounded and didn't know how dire the situation was, he began to run the opposite way of which they threw him, shoving past spirits as they carved their nails into his sides.

For Paul, it wasn't helpful that he was deep in the corridor, yanked by a man in a wall, then shoved out, and turned around. He was lost and it seemed like he couldn't go through the spirits, as he wasn't able to walk through them. Stumbling and tripping from the loss of stamina, Paul instinctively collapsed into a class to catch his breath and to his surprise, there were bodies and blood everywhere.

Scattered on the ground, hung from the ceiling, nailed to the wall, there were corpses and pieces of corpses littered the room. It was sickening as the smell of the rotting bodies struck Paul's nose like a homing missile. Backing himself against a wall to take in all that he's seen or heard, trying to understand all of the horrors that laid within his position.

He held his right hand to his mouth tightly as he gagged, trying to swallow the puke that attempted to make acquaintances with the floor. The horrid smell mixed with the taste of the throw up, made him barf up food he didn't know he ate.

"What the hell is this place, what in the world is going on?" he thought to himself as his thoughts raced. He stared at the ground as his survival instincts were beginning to set in, losing a bit of sanity every second. "If this is what people do," his head turned to his right and saw a fire axe sitting on a desk. "Then why shouldn't I be a protector for the rest of my life?" He questioned as he grabbed the axe, it was his favorite weapon in video games. "If I can't push through them then maybe I can slice them, wait," he pondered as he realized an idea that made sense. He raised the axe high above his head with his right hand, heavily striking himself in his left arm. As soon as he gashes himself, he pulled the axe out of his arm.

"Shit!" he screamed as he looked at the bloody gape in his arm. "So this isn't a dream, then maybe I'm dead. I could be in a paradox, gah, that wouldn't make sense," he mumbled as he began to bang his head against the wall to bite the pain.

He knew there was no time to rest and that he needed to get outside of the school as soon as possible. He stood up with the axe in hand, and walked towards the exit. He stared at the door handle, questioning himself as to if he should move on.

"If only I could find the end to this hell hall," he thought as he grabbed the door handle and opened the door towards himself slowly.

The hinges creaked from the rust as he peeked his head into the hall, it was empty and dark, but Paul knew that he wasn't alone. He began to pace himself down the hall, slowly walking with the axe handle in one hand and the axe neck in the other. The blade pointed outwards, away from himself. He had no idea if he could kill these spirits, but he was ready to put up a fight. It was as if he were always meant for this moment, to survive for the fate of whatever he had to figure out later.

The sounds of weeping filled the halls as the doors rapidly swung and the lights flickered in the hallway like a flashing alarm. Doors brushed his body as he rushed down the hall as he made sure to empty his mind.

He whipped around corners to meet dead ends, traveling back to the hallway he left, he began to walk further and further away from the stairwell. Paul walked in the endless hallway for what seemed like five minutes until he met a dead end on the straight path. The screams and horrors that affected Paul mentally, silenced themselves as he approached the distorted dead end.

"Well," his thoughts began to rush back to him like a football team as he stared at the distortion. "Looks as if the only way out is turning around," he thought in horror as he slowly turned around. There was nothing, not even a light flickering in the dark hallway he was consumed in. "Where are the spirits?" He asked himself as he looked around the dark hallway.

Thinking that it was just an illusion, he turned around to retrace his steps when he felt a flesh-like hand tugging at the arm that held the axe handle. Seeing a spirit hanging halfway out of the wall, he attempted to yank his arm away, but the spirit wouldn't let go.

"Help us," he heard the spirit say, its voice stressed and horrid.

He whipped around to see that the dead end of the hallway was beginning to warp itself, as if it were made of some bubble. Realizing it wasn't an illusion, he finally ripped his arm from the spirits grip as he concentrated on the distortion

The spirit retreated back into the dark wall as Paul ignored it, walking over to the distorted wall. Noticing there was something solid when he kicked his foot to the base of the wall, he heard the knock his shoe made against its hard wood.

"This isn't a wall nor a discontinued hallway, and it's definitely not a mirror. It looks like some distorted door," he thought as he put his hand through it, immediately retreating it to his chest as he felt an extreme heat. "There seems to be a distortion between what connects this world to another, it's all fiery and yet so cold," he concluded as he put his hand in front of his face.

Inspecting it by rolling it around, he saw that it was almost burnt to a crisp when he suddenly heard a girl's cry from behind him, causing him to lose interest in his burnt hand.

Turning his attention to that area with the axe still wielded, he began creeping towards the cry that periodically stopped. The closer he got, the more it sounded like a sob, then sinister laughter. The hallway felt so dense, as if millions of distressed souls were watching him. Paul crept, keeping an eye out for anything out of the normal until he stood in front of a regular classroom door with a single light above. A cry was heard just inside of the classroom, begging him for help.

The distorted wall stood about fifty feet down the hallway, staring ill-intently at Paul. He gripped the knob and twisted it, opening the door slowly to reveal a dark narrow hall that led into a larger room. A red string laid on the ground, crawling down the narrow hallway to the back of the large room. The smell of old water and putrid rotting bodies hit Paul's nose as he followed the string, staying next to it as he walked and inspected the dark room.

Water was leaking from the ceiling, creating a puddle just to his right. He entered the larger room and for a school classroom, this room was huge. The walls curved outwards as they surrounded the room, there were decorations hung up as if for someone's birthday and glass laid scattered across the floor. Baby dolls hung across the walls on strings, some were burnt and missing parts. It began to freak Paul out, but his adrenaline overpowered his fear.

"This could be a trap," he cautioned to himself as he began to think. "There's glass on the floor but no windows. Maybe there was a party and it got interrupted. Look at me," he chuckled at himself as he stared straight ahead. "Look at me trying to figure out the post apocalypse of this place." He stopped in front of a black board, scribbles were everywhere and no words were legible.

"If this is the end of the room," he thought as he looked to his left and right, seeing that the walls were barely visible. "Then where's the crying coming from? It surely was," he thought as they were interrupted by a cry much louder than the first time, as if it were in his left ear.

He snapped his attention to his left as a light flicked on, revealing a girl about Pauls' size and age that sat against the curved wall. A light flicked onto her face, blinding her eyes, revealing that she was obviously not supposed to be on this floor. He approached her carefully, as if she were going to attack, Paul picked up the flashlight that laid next to her, gently. He wielded the axe to his left side with his left hand gripping the neck.

Suddenly, she looked up and began to stare deeply into Paul's eyes and he could see that she wasn't a spirit, she was a petrified human. She wore a black robe with the hood down, revealing her long black hair and orange eyes. She had her back against the wall, afraid of what Paul might try to do. It seemed as if she were trying to get further away.

"Hey," Paul gently proposed as he placed the flashlight next to himself on his right. He extended his right hand towards her, attempting to build trust. "I'm not an enemy, are you?" He smiled gently, as if to try and comfort her.

She began to reach her hand towards him when her hand balled up into a fist, with only her index pointing out. She began to shudder and Paul could see the fear rise in her eyes. He turned around quickly, picking up the flashlight. He shined his light behind himself to reveal a wall on the other side of the room.

"It's behind the wall," her soft voice trembled as she spoke.

"Does it notice us?" he asked, gripping the neck of the axe in his left hand.

Fear began to creep into his mind as he pointed his flashlight towards the wall. The room was so big, the entrance narrowed into a decent sized circle. He didn't know the size nor the danger of his enemy, but Paul knew he had to protect this girl. He began to tie the string on the flashlight to his belt buckle, dropping the light to the floor, causing his shoes to light up.

"Shit," he thought. "What to do? If I make the wrong move, then a chase will be initiated. I can't carry her and outrun him, but I can attempt to fight," he thought as he realized his situation, putting his feet into his favorite, the tree chopper position. He began to wield the axe as before, tightly in both hands, but with the blade behind him as he stood sideways.

"Alright," he gulped down some air, gently letting it out. He began to think about how lumberjacks swung their axes, putting all of their power into their feet. "If it's bigger than me," he calmly thought. "Try to out maneuver it. If the problem gets too big, run."

Realizing the only option to lure the enemy towards him, he began to scream to the top of his lungs to get its attention. His voice echoed the empty hallway like a yodeler on a mountain peak. To Paul's horror, it worked.

Emerging from the wall, sending drywall flying, a seven-foot figure with a blade bigger than itself roared so loud it shook the building. It didn't have a face but just a singular eye where his facial features should have been. Its arms were long and stood at about Paul's size. He wore no clothes but a black cult robe, he seemed to be a demon from another dimension. It took a step forward as Paul shook in his shoes as to what might come next.

"What the hell are you?" Paul asked as he took a step backwards, stunned by horror as the girl rushed behind him for protection. Paul felt himself gain courage, as if he was falling asleep.

It swung its sword at the two, nearly splitting them in half as Paul grabbed the girl and moved themselves out of the way to the right. The ground split from the blow as Paul and the girl ran towards the entrance of the circle. They ran out of the room with the girl dragging along behind him as the being followed them slowly down the hall like a killer.

"I'm going to put you somewhere," Paul puffed through breaths as he took a left into a dead end.

He placed her down, supporting her back against the wall.

"I know this is going to sound like a cliché, but stay there until I get back."

She looked up at him with hope in her eyes and gave a single nod as he sprinted down the hallway. Doors began to open and close rapidly as spirits of children appeared in the hall, grabbing at Paul.

Paul yanked himself away to avoid being slowed down, their flesh was sticky and gooey. The spirits began to wail, like a high-pitched moan from a whale suffering. There were so many that the noises began to bother Paul, he had to get somewhere safe. His thoughts began to bother him as the screams were beginning to affect him mentally. He jumped off to his right side through a door, wood flew off from the impact.

He landed, sliding on his side as a crack was to be heard from the right arm that still wielded the axe. Blood began to leak onto the floor as he began to stand up. A hand was felt on his shoulder, shoving him back onto the ground. He looked up in shock and horror, expecting his end.

The girl with orange eyes stood above him with worry in her eyes, examining his body as she began to stare at his bloody arm. It went limp as he stood up and brushed her off, dropping the axe. The screams began to fade into silence as they stood in the dark room. He began to rush around the room, picking up desks and placing them into a specified corner.

"It'll be here soon," he assured them both as he began to make a barrier in the corner of the room out of the desks he's placed.

"Get in here, you'll be safe. The only way we can freely think is to get rid of that thing, and if I run my mind will be rushed with thoughts about whether he's behind me or not. You might be a spirit, I don't know, but I'm just going to say that you're human. I want to get you out of here just as much as I want out of here. Do you understand?"

She nodded in agreement and began to crawl into the tiny hole Paul made out of desks and chairs.

"It may not be the safest nor the best hiding spot, but it's a hiding spot. It was made in a rush and…" he was interrupted by a loud crash. He turned to his right, covering his face with his limp arm as chunks of wall flew across the room. As they landed, a few pieces of the wall got stuck into his arm, causing him to bleed more. His eyes were filled with sawdust, fear, and determination.

The being grabbed Paul by the arm, throwing him towards the entrance of the room. Quickly picking up his axe before being launched, Paul lost his grip on the axe, causing it to fly out of his hand and slide towards the far left side of the room. It approached him slowly, standing like a giant over the now lying down Paul. The beings sword dragged behind him as it scraped the tile floor. Its' arms were very thick with what looked to be fat and muscle from carrying the sword. Seeing it in the light, this thing was more horrifying than ever. Its singular eye didn't have lids so they never blinked.

The being swung his sword with one arm towards the petrified Paul, slicing a hole through the wall behind him. The sword crashed into the ground, causing it to break and fold. Paul was tossed to the right side of the room when the floor folded, crashing his back into the wall with a thud and crack. His head went limp as his mouth coughed up blood.

The demon slowly turned his head towards his victim Paul, who was curled up in a bloody ball as he began to move, his body aching with every movement as the blood leaked from his body. Paul struggled to get to his feet, his legs shook with the weight of his body pressuring them.

He stabilized his legs and began to sprint towards the far left side of the room, to where his axe was. The being stomped, lifting everything that touched the floor. Paul braced and used the momentum from the stomp to shoot himself over the monster towards the left side of the room, grabbing his axe as he tumbled and rolled.

His lungs burned with every breath he took, forgetting how many bones were actually broken. He began to feel sleepy but shook it off as if him needing to survive was the only way out. The being roared and began to charge at Paul, its shoulder ready to squish him against the wall.

Paul braced as he put his axe long ways close to his chest preparing for impact. They collided, sending him backwards into the wall, but still remained on his feet. The shoulder of the giant stood against Paul's axe struggling to push forward. He struggled to hold the being back, pushing it with all of the energy and strength he had left.

Suddenly, he spun around the side of the beast, releasing the axe from its confrontation. As he spun, so did the axe, landing a deep blow into the back of the demon near the spine, making it screech in pain. He removed his axe and stepped back to get himself room.

"It can scream?" Paul thought as he stood a distance away from the being that's crouching down, aiding to its back. "But where is its mouth, wait, I can't give him time to recover." He burst into action, swinging the axe towards the now turning beast, its head was in perfect striking position. It landed in its eye, causing blood to spurt as it was shut close from the blade being yanked out. It grabbed its eye, causing the being to drop his sword and begin crawling around in pain.

Paul wielded the axe high over his head, his arms shaking from the loss of blood. With the blade pointed towards the ceiling, he planted his right foot on its back for stabilization. Blood dripped off from the tip as he crashed it down onto the back of its neck, snapping the axe in two. The axe was stuck in its neck and the beast stopped squirming, falling silent.

He panted as he walked backwards, falling onto his ass gagging from the smell and from the fact he just killed something.

"How could I?" He thought. "It's not like me to kill anything," he tensed up as he tried to move, but it was nearly impossible. "I have to get her and leave, it's our only option."

Paul stammered to his feet as determination was keeping his body from aching. Stumbling with every step he took, his knees kept locking up and his right arm was severely broken due to ignoring the fracture during the fight. He walked up to the hole he made for his ally and kneeled down to look inside, resting his left arm on his left knee.

"You okay?" he asked softly in short breaths.

She nodded, pointing at his arm asking if he was okay. He nodded as if not to converse for too long, Paul didn't know if the demon was actually dead, or even what it was.

He turned around and bent down, pointing towards his back to signal her to climb on. She climbed out of the hole and climbed onto his back with a smile on her face.

"Hold on," he commanded towards the kid.

She nodded as he turned around and approached the demon that still laid on the ground. He wanted to grab his axe but his arm was too damaged to even twitch a finger, let alone carry this kid. Even if he did pick it up with his free hand, he would need the other to hold her.

Turning around, Paul stepped over the wood that lay scattered on the floor, entering the hallway. He looked both to his left and right, there was no clear end on either side. The mirror was nowhere to be seen as he took the path on the left as blood still dripped from his arm. They walked for what seemed like an hour in silence as they walked towards the mirror.

"Do you know what this is?" Paul asked the girl as they stared at their distorted reflection.

She nodded her head, "It's a door to my home."

His eyes widened with shock, "Could she really be from another dimension?" Paul asked himself.

"Tell me," he wondered as he was kneeling down and setting her onto her feet. He let his body go limp against the wall on his left, looking more pale every second. "Who are you anyway? I'm not going to ask multiple questions, so just tell me everything please." he urged as he rested his head against the wall and gave an exhausted sigh.

"My name is Gwen," she expressed her words in a more proper tone than before, as if her voice had less fear in it. She watched Paul slide down the wall before continuing, letting him get comfortable.

"I escaped my father through that window between this world and the next. He used to abuse me, yet I heard so many stories about the above world and wanted to explore. How beautiful it was, how large and expansive it was. They told of people who were kind, they talked about love and peace. So I asked my father if I could go to the above world, but he denied me. He predicted that the people in the above world was wicked, sick, and everything terrible.

"I've always hated my father for he tortured me since birth, so I escaped. Ending up here, the hallway was so long, I got lost. My father's henchman came looking for me before I could make it to the third door. I ran inside of a room, hiding until he found me and chased me through a vent into the room you found me in. That's all I know. Oh," she stopped and stared at her hands, twirling her thumbs. "My father is known as the watcher over the underworld, my mother is a human demon. Apparently, she was a part of a crew that got abducted into the underworld and tortured. I heard only one person made it out alive, and I will avenge her," she remembered in anger.

"So, how old are you?" Paul asked as if he had nothing else to say.

"I think in the underworld I'm two hundred and twenty-six hours old. There aren't any days, just hours. For every hour in the underworld, a month passes in your world."

"That's a lot of hours," he bantered, chuckling at the absurdity of the situation. "We've gotta go, I've thought about it," he asserted, standing up but stumbling back down from the pain in his legs.

Gwen knelt down to aid in help as she grabbed his bloody arm with one hand and took off her shoe with the next. Her foot was covered with a black silky sock, she slipped it off stretching it to its max.

"It's pretty stretchy," she attempted to make small talk. "I don't know much about humans, but after breaking almost every bone in my body, I've learned some aiding. Like how to neutralize poison and how to fix anything from a small crack to a break or a fracture." She lifted his arm, inspecting it and squishing it as he winced in pain.

"You've completely shattered your arm. There's no repair but therapy, so I'm going to need to stay alongside you while you heal." She gave him a soft smile as she wrapped her sock around his now folded arm, extending it behind his neck and back to the beginning. She squeezed a tough knot into the sock to secure the bandage and healing.

"You couldn't be more gentle?" Paul annoyingly asked.

"I didn't know the mortal who took down one of Satins' henchmen felt pain," she jokingly snapped back.

"Wait," he grabbed her hand in shock. "You're Satan's' child?" his eyes were wide with excitement. He's always wanted to meet other worldly beings, at that Satan's child.

"Yeah. Don't get overly excited, I'm not going back. And if you think about going through that portal, don't. If you enter, you will be torn apart if you're not a dead soul. Meaning, if you have a flesh bag on, you may not enter."

"So what," Paul began to think. "Do I just turn around and find the principle, or just act like none of this happened? And hold on, for being the devil's child, she's surprisingly happy."

Suddenly a roar filled the entire hallway, sending chills down both of their spines.

"It looked like you killed it," Gwen began in horror when the gigantic monster began to barrel down the hall. The robe he wore was gone, revealing a black charred and cracked body. A ragged mouth was seen on his chest, and tons of fire leaked from the multiple cracks. "

"I've got an idea," she proposed as she placed her hand onto his chest. "As long as you're with me," she prepared herself as she closed her eyes, causing a bright glow around her. "You will always be safe."

With the monster inches behind them, she projected an aura upon Paul before quickly grabbing his collar, yanking them both into the pool of distortion.

Landing in a fiery area, Gwen realized a mistake she hadn't noticed before. The location of the portal was moved, as if the destination was purposely changed.

She got up, brushing the dirt from her pants. She began inspecting her body for injuries as she looked at her arms.

"Do you need help?" she asked, extending her hand.

Paul grabbed it with the single hand he had left and lifted himself to his feet with her support. He brushed off the dirt on his shoulders and looked around. They stood in the middle of a huge arena of fire, and cries of weeping souls were heard from every direction which they stood.

"Where are we?" he asked Gwen as he pulled out his phone to inspect it and to his surprise, it showed a bunch of lines that stretched from one side of his smartphone to the other.

"Welcome to my hometown, Hell." she presented with exciting hate. "There should be a group of guards to greet us here soon."

"I thought you said they weren't friendly, why would they be here to 'greet' us?"

"There's no need to get tense, stop taking everything so seriously. I understand you have to rely on your guard when you're in your house, but around me there is no guard." She got in his face, getting on her toes and putting a finger in front of it. "Got it," she sternly stated.

He shook his head in agreement, thinking this chick might be crazy.

"As I was saying," she returned to her feet and folded her arms. "Yes they are brutal, but I'm the princess. That means if they harm me or anyone I say to not harm, they get the highest punishment. Which is just being smothered in candy, imagine loving so much hate to be covered by sugar. It surprisingly burns the skin off of guard demons and yet there are demons that would enjoy that.

"Regular demons would enjoy the smell, taste, sight, and even the feel, these are the ones that lived on the surface and were convicted down to here. There are torture demons, though not large in numbers, they handle the small tortures. Satin himself has the power to put those he wants in an infinite loop of death. I was caught in one and escaped, that's why I retreated to the mortal world."

Paul stood there, trying to absorb the information she was telling him. Knowing so much of this was beginning to be overwhelming to him, he had to sit down.

"And the ones coming for us now are the guards, demons that were born down here and raised by Satin. They have never seen the light of day, nor the light of the above world. The ceilings here are just a layer of fire, well, technically there is no ceiling. It's just a bunch of never ending fire until you reach the middle where you end up in the waiting room to wait for your sentencing."

She put her flat hand over her eyebrows if she were blocking the sun from her eyes. There were about a hundred demons seen on the horizon with a single being that blocked most of the army.

"Here they come, and if you look in the front, you can see my dad."

Intense fear began to build in Paul as he looked up from his seat in horror. "What the hell am I doing here?" Paul began rapidly thinking as Gwen rambled on about a vase she had broken and hid from her father. "Okay, a lot's going on. First," he put his head on his hand, propping it up on his knee. "My friend had to pee and I had to get dragged into going on the wrong floor. Why did I have to follow? Second, an arm appeared out of darkness and grabbed me. Turns out it was the janitor that was actually a, what did he call it? Think, think."

He began to tap on his chin while the army slowly moved towards them. Gwen was still rambling on about the things she's broken and how she had to hide them from her parents as Paul stared at the serpent like creature that was now closer.

"Did you hear anything I said?" Gwen turned around to ask Paul, looking him in the face.

Startled, Paul snapped out of his thoughts and chuckled nervously. "Yeah, honestly up to the part where you were talking about breaking things. It's honestly a lot of information to take in but I understand. What you're saying is that there's a difference in torture when it comes to certain demons, but are you sure your dad isn't going to kill me?" He asked, his voice trembling.

"Well maybe, if the idea I have works then we should be fine. Whatever you do, just go with what I say. Okay?"

The army was within earshot when wheels were heard as burning carriages and horses approached them. Demon soldiers sat upon the cart with a whip in hand, commanding the horses to move faster. The giant in front stood about the ceiling of Hell, his face was unseen as it was in the fire. He began to shrink, his entire body singulated to one point at his center. He wore no shoes yet had lizard-like feet, and the suit that covered his massively built chest was bright red. A fresh white shirt was tucked under his black tie as he smiled like a gremlin when he spoke.

"Daughter," he uttered in a deep tone, almost too deep to understand. "Leaving and disobeying my orders is restricted. You are going to need torture to keep you straight." He reached out and grabbed Gwen by the arm, dragging her as he walked away.

Paul grabbed Gwen by the shoe with his left arm, yanking her back with small force.

"Let her go," Paul challenged bravely as he stood there feeling dumb for what he's done.

Turning around and dropping her arm, Satin approached Paul. His grin made Paul want to turn and run away, but somehow he swallowed his fear as she collapsed to the ground face first, making Paul drop her foot.

"You." Every word sent shivered down his spine as he grumbled. "Who do you think you are?" he asked, expecting an answer quickly. His breath made Paul's nose want to shrivel and disappear.

"I'm a mere mortal compared to you, so I cannot ask a lot." Paul choked.

Satin began to chuckle and laugh loudly, causing the entire army to fall under a laughing spell. The laughter filled the entire surrounding area, making rocks fall and crumble onto the ground. He stopped and so did the army, instantaneously.

"Fight my army mortal," he bargained as he presented his army with a swift extension of his arm, turning his body sideways. "Put up a decent fight and you win my daughter at a cost, isn't that why you're here?"

"Shit," Paul thought as sweat poured from his face. "Did the devil of all men just challenge me, ME!" He crushed his hand making his arm tense up as he realized this wasn't a fair fight. "I'm just a mere mortal against what I can only say is an army of immortals. If my studying in this subject were for anything, I could use it now. Though the only other option is to. Gah, why am I thinking?" He arose to his feet, ready for a bloody brawl.

"If you want to know the truth, I was basically dragged here," he explained, spitting out the remaining blood that was stuck in his lung. His broken arm spilled blood through the sock as it stung with pain, he lifted his left fist into the air to block his face. There was blood dripping from Paul's left hand as well.

"I just wanted to go to school, go home, and go to sleep. Now, I'm stuck trying to rescue someone in danger and I didn't even wanna jump into this damn place. Discussing my problems with the devil who couldn't give a shit about them isn't helping either." Paul shifted his shoulders, pointing the left one towards his enemy. "So, if this gets me home, I'll do it."

He began to charge, running past Satin towards the demon to his left, he dodged a swift swing from the demon guard's black axe. He jumped upwards towards the demon's face as it struggled to pull its blade out of the ground. He grabbed its head with his good arm and spun himself around, twisting it off like a cap on a bottle. Paul landed on one knee with his hand to the ground and head down as the head bounced to rest at the demon's army feet.

Turning around, the army began to surround Paul, jumping on him all at once. They kicked, punched, and stabbed for what seemed like hours, until the devil raised a hand. The army backed away slowly, revealing a shattered Paul lying in his own blood.

"You have shown me enough mere mortal," he laughed in pleasure as he began walking towards him. Looking down at his feet, he could see the broken Paul coughing.

"I know what holds your future, and I cannot stand in the way for I will be erased along with everything I own. Guards," he pointed to the men closest to him. "Take them away, and if I ever see them down here again, they both die," he glared.

A guard picked up Paul and put him onto their shoulder. Gwen walked freely and as they began to leave, Satin cursed them.

"You will be followed by my guards everyday of your life, no matter how long you live. That is my deal," he offered before turning around and walking the way they came.

"You really got the short end of the stick, mortal." The guard's voice was deep and it stood at seven foot eight inches. "If you weren't so special to the man upstairs, then he'd have killed you. Do not come back," he warned as they reached another mirror. The guard put Paul onto his long, skinny forearm and threw him through.

Gwen watched as the demon launched Paul through the portal, probably breaking more bones. She approached the mirror after the guard moved aside, letting her enter through the portal. Paul flew through the mirror back into the school as Gwen nonchalantly walks through. The portal closed behind them, leaving them in a dark hallway.

"What the hell," Paul stammered.

"Well," Gwen began. "I guess we're stuck together from now on." she expressed as she got to her feet and she stared down the narrow pitch black hallway. She picked up Paul, who was nearly unconscious, and cradled him in her arms. She carried him down the hallway to the stairwell he began at.

"You're lucky to be breathing, do you know where the hospital is?" She asked as she began looking around at the dark walls. She thought it was best to keep on the straight path.

Gwen walked for what seemed like a few minutes before being met with a steel door. The gray tag next to the door read: STAIRS. She opened the heavy door with one hand and began to walk down the steps towards the exit. Her hair bounced as she panted down the stairs, stabilizing her breathing.

Paul was amazed by her strength, it made him wonder how much she could really handle. "Maybe," he began to think while curled up in Gwens arms. "Maybe I should be an omni-verse protector," he mumbled before passing out.

Chapter 5

Seans Beginning

"Hey, we need those burgers out here quick." Adam, the manager of Winky Wacky Burgers, shouted as he nimbly avoided every table and customer to not drop the food that he was delivering to the hungry folk. He stood short with blonde hair and a soft face.

The tables were filled with hungry customers and the kitchen was furiously cooking as their sweat made puddles on the ground. The Winky Wacky Burgers is one of four restaurants in Skylark. Being at the top in its class, everyone enjoyed visiting the Winky Wacky Burgers for its name and tasty food.

"I need to make a re-up on wings," yelled Sean, a slim and tall man with black hair. "The burgers are on the grill, they'll be up in a minute!" he yelled as he disappeared into the storage room.

Sean works early morning until late night, making above the minimum wage of four dollars an hour. He lived alone in a small apartment on the fifth floor with a cat and a bulldog. His life wasn't a total wreck anymore and though he had student debts from The Skylark Everything School's college, he enjoyed everything he did.

From working at a fast food chain to watching Netflix, to sharing popcorn with his dog, he had very little to worry about. He could be famous but he wasn't good at anything people would approve of.

He walked to the hefty refrigerator door and pulled on the handle, pulling it open with a heave and a ho. Sean always kept calm during lunch time or dinner rushes, he was the man everyone in the business relied on. He stepped into the open cooler where all of the refrigerated food was stored, and approached the freezer door. He pulled it open as tons of frost and smoke poured out, embodying Sean in its cool air.

"Where are those burgers?" he thought as he walked around the cold room, scanning the materials in the freezer. "Ah," he thought as he picked up a one-hundred percent beef patty box and walked it back to the kitchen. He placed it in a small freezer next to his grill and slit the tape off with a box cutter he kept on himself.

Sean rushed to the now steaming grill. "Did nobody take the burgers off?" He asked angrily as he shuffled the spatula against the charcoal meat. It made him wonder why he wastes his breath to slackers.

The rest of the evening went by smoothly, it was busy until near closing time but everybody was served and was happy. Adam walked to the back of the kitchen to talk to Sean.

"It was surely a rush today wasn't it?" he asked as he motioned for Sean to walk outside by pulling out his lighter.

"It was, the kitchen crew could barely keep up," Sean complained as they stood outside, pulling a cigarette from their boxes. They lit their cigarettes and began to finish their conversation.

"Did you hear what Sasha did?" Adam bickered as smoke leaked from his mouth. "She spilled a table of six's food and then ran off to the bathroom."

Street lights kept the night darkness away from the parking lot ahead of them. It was empty and large; nearly four hundred cars could fit due to the massive shopping center in front of the building.

"Maybe she didn't mean to," he argued, flicking the ash from his cigarette, landing in a puddle nearby.

"I mean I understand accidents happen but she could have cleaned it up. I mean she stayed there until the business died down, but still," flicking his cigarette, he looked up to see something arcing towards them. "What the fuc-"

Sean, looking down at the grease on his shoe and laces, looked up to see the object barreling towards them. He put his hands up over his head, guarding himself. It landed into the roof of the restaurant, causing a big crash that sent wood and steel shards flying.

"Woah!" Sean yelled as he made a twirl into the street at an angle, putting his left hand behind him and his right foot still on the curb. His right arm was guarding his chest, along with his left foot on the black top, as he stared at the fresh massive hole in the restaurant roof.

"What the hell was that," asked Adam as he rushed to the door, flinging it open and running inside.

Sean rushed in behind as his heart raced like a car, he followed his manager. Laid before them was wood and steel folding to a center on the ground that held a man in a red and black vertically striped hood. He wore a solid red mask that covered everything but the eyes, and his jeans were ripped. He sat up and began to be fixated on where he came from. Fire erupted in the kitchen as a gas leak occurred, causing a small explosion in the behind the appalled man.

"Who the hell," Adam began to say when the man stood up, still staring at the ceiling. "Look at me, do you know what you just did?"

Sean watched as Adam approached him, angrily waving his right fist in the air as he screamed. The man stood motionless as he stared through the hole in the ceiling towards the sky. He got close enough to grab his shirt, yanking him and looking him in the eye.

"Hold on Adam," Sean mumbled with recognition in his voice. "I might know him."

Suddenly, a short girl wearing a solid black mask skipped in. She wore more black than pink shoulder to toe, along with a pink bookbag on her back. She briskly walked past Sean and approached Adam, putting a hand on his shoulder. Her voice was sweet but scary.

"Hey, I don't know who you are, but take your hands off of him. I don't want it to be uglier than it already is," she warned as Adam turned his head to look her in the eyes. He lost his grip on the man, trembling with nothing but fear in his eyes.

Letting him go, he began to scream and hold his hands to the sides of his head as he fell to his knees. He began to cite a demon prayer as he tore flesh from his face. Blood began to pour as he continued throughout his entire body, leaving nothing but a man with holes and muscles.

"What the fuck did you do?" Sean asked as he ran over to comfort Adam.

"You must be of importance to him," she whispered as she knelt next to him. "We need you," before standing up to walk over to the stunned man.

Suddenly, the blares of sirens began to fill the night, echoing throughout the city. The man began to speak, his tone was sincere.

"I'm sorry for the loss, but we need you Sean. The omni-verses depend on you to be the leader of its protectors." They suddenly leaped through the hole in the ceiling, disappearing into the night sky.

Sean ran outside looking around for the two as fire trucks and ambulances were the first on the scene, along with some annoyed neighbors. They almost flipped their vehicles as they approached, whipping around tight corners. Firemen rushed into the building with hoses, spraying the fire at its base. Paramedics stood by, waiting for the firemen to finish their jobs. Police cars rushed in five minutes later.

A police officer wearing a mostly orange outfit and black boots, walked up to Sean. He pulled out a notepad and pen from his shirt pocket that had the name "David," written on it.

"Do you know what happened here?" he asked as he chewed on his gum, annoyed.

Seans expression went blank as he stared into space and began to have a flashback, completely removing him from reality.

Paul and Sean were next to each other in the living room at Lucyfers house. He stood there as the beings played out in front of them slowly. They were talking, toys were scattered about and wrapping paper was stuffed in a gigantic trash bag.

"This was Christmas of twenty eleven, I just got my first phone. Why am I here?" Sean began to remember, beginning to think.

A being appeared floating in the kitchen not too far away from him as Lucyfer sat in the chair at the top of the counter in a swivel chair. It was short and looked like an angelic troll.

"You are in your past," he explained. His voice was comforting for a troll, too comforting. "These are the times you loved the most."

He began floating around the room towards Sean, who stood behind the couches. The living room and kitchen were conjoined into a singular room, along with what they called the sun room. The only thing that separated the kitchen from the sun room was a wall that sat upon the counter next to the island counter. On the far left, facing the island counter, sat a black fridge that held a Thanksgiving like feast.

Sean stood next to the couch where the carpet met the tile floor with a metal outline.

"Let me ask my questions before we proceed or I'm going to get out of here," Sean argued as he stood in the living room, not too far away from the creature.

"You can ask your questions if you'd like, I'm patient," he replied as he hovered in one spot, folding his arms. "However, there is no way you can escape this memory before I tell you what I shall tell you. This is your destined purpose presented by The Creator."

"The Creator?" Sean whispered.

"If you don't remember the book then I can tell you. He is the one who created the universe you stand in, and every other unknown universe out there. Truth of the matter is, he's always building his infinite universe, and in reality, there is no end or beginning to his universe. There are however, boundaries that we as watchers and protectors use.

"Even mere humans know about this ideology that we use, so it's pretty easy to understand. Basically, a universe is a cluster of one or more galaxies that eventually turns into a multiverse, which henceforth creates an omni-verse from a cluster, or group, of multiverses And let's not get started on the demi-verse that holds sleeping demons."

"What?" Sean asked, puzzled. "I'm not entirely following."

"Right, I'll explain," the spirit put a hand under his chin as he thought. "Basically the universe that we live in is technically a galaxy with an alternate galaxy timeline, making our or any universe. So, when there are two or more universes in a collection of a singular spot, it's known to turn into a multiverse that consists of multiple universes."

It began to make sense for Sean as he pieced the puzzle together.

"So what I'm guessing is that a collection of more than one or two multiverses makes an omni-verse," Sean understood, snapping his finger

"Exactly," the spirit cheerfully yelled. "So, the one who created these omni-verses put a man in charge of watching over them day and night. He is known as the High Priest and is also known to have courage, bravery, and a clean soul. As to every being, there is an alternative to him known as the Low Priest. He's the one Satin has appointed to try and destroy what the one above is creating. Now listen, neither the High Priest nor the Low Priest are allowed on any planet, unless their ki is lower than zero.

"So in order to do anything but watch, he hired four followers to fight on his behalf. They represented hope throughout every omni-verse, though one day there was a fight in a universe where Satin captured three of his warriors. It's been months since we've made contact with the last follower, leaving the omni-verses in shambles.

"Wars began to break out, destroying practically everything. They feared nothing from anybody anymore, and I'm afraid they won't ever be afraid again. Though everything changed just a few weeks ago when the High Priest got a message from his last follower, he resigned without hesitation. The grief that overtook him made him quit since one of the other followers was his wife."

Sean stood there, trying to unscramble the information in his head. "What're you saying?" he stammered.

"We have little time," the spirit ushered. "All in all, we need replacements for the warriors we've lost. Four loyal people who have nothing to live for, to put in the plainest."

"There's no way," he thought in shock.

"I have to go, but know this before I leave. When the time comes, you will have to defeat the Low Priest." the spirit whispered as it disappeared into the air. The flashback began to fade as red and blue lights blinded Sean everywhere he looked.

"Where am I?" Sean asked the officer, confused.

"I said, do you know what happened here?" The gum was still being grinded in the officers mouth as he talked, annoyed

"Some dude came in through the ceiling," he pointed towards the hole. "He kind of just came out of nowhere. There was another person but both people…"

A deep roar was heard not too far away, along with a huge explosion that sent chunks of bricks and houses into the air. The officer flew his arms over his head and crouched down as a car zipped by right above his head. Sean, who was on the curb, stood up and began to panic.

"What the hell," he asked himself as he began to rush towards the explosion.

His heart raced as he couldn't believe what he was doing. He sped off across the street towards the front yards to the back right of the restaurant. More explosions burst out in flames as he crossed the road and ran to his left, towards the road that split the clustered houses in half. He was getting closer and closer the further he went towards the back of the street. He approached a fence that led to a few baseball fields and jumped it, like he used to in his military days. Motion sensor lights lit up the dark, revealing wet grass from the rain.

"Who was that man?" he wondered as laid onto the wet grass to conceal himself.

A woman, a man, and a beast were in a standoff. The man stood in front of the woman while the beast towered the two, who were holding weapons.

"Are those baseball bats?" Sean curiously asked himself as he squinted not too far from the gate entrance.

Sean laid about fifty feet away from the scene, slowly creeping and crawling towards the three. His shoes lightly squeaked against the grass as he pressed his feet against the grass to hide himself. He stopped at about twenty feet from the group, his chin touched where the grass ended and the dirt began. Overhead lights shone brightly throughout the field and now he could clearly see now that the man was holding a sword. The demon was holding a long handle with a big curved red blade that touched the ground. They began to talk;

"I'm here to make sure to end you," began the demonic creature.

"You're here to be sent back," the man threatened, pointing his sword towards the demon. "I'm not here for discussion."

The female stood behind the man, a pink bat lazily sat in her hand. She was short and wore a mask.

"That's them," Sean thought. "They were at the restaurant when it collapsed. Maybe that demon has something to do with it."

He watched as the man and demon charged each other, their weapons clashed as they began to counter each other's attacks. They began to move around the field at a rapid pace, moving faster and faster as their swings became invisible. It was as if they were floating as they furiously clashed weapons. Blood was spilled after a cut was seen every now and then from both of them.

The man was sent flying backwards, landing onto his feet. He stood about twenty feet away as he charged the demon, but the demon struck the scythe to the ground, causing it to crack and interrupt his thought. He jumped backwards towards the female, landing on his back as he lost his footing, causing dirt to swirl in the air as he rolled to a stop. He lost control of his sword when he jumped backwards, causing it to fly to his right.

"Do you think that you can defeat me?" The demon taunted as it slowly walked towards the man with its scythe in its left hand.

He coughed and replied, "It's not that I cannot defeat you." He jumped to his feet with his sword not too far away. "If you look at it, you can easily throw me off of my guard by tossing me. It's very effective for everyone, that's why I hate it."

Suddenly he began to run, slipping under the demon's legs towards the sword that lay waiting for a user. He picked up the weapon and began to charge the demon's back with the one handed sword, the demon responded with a ground pound to counter his original attack again. Using the ground pound as momentum to throw him into the air, the man launched himself from the demon's axe and slowly flipped forward using the sword's weight. He threw the demon off of his guard, bringing down the heavy sword onto the demon's head, causing a deep gash into its skull.

"You don't waste time huh?" the female asked as the man crumbled to the ground.

"We've gotta go, someone's been watching." The man spoke in confidence as he stood up and began to walk towards the corpse of the demon.

He lifted his sword and thumped it down, cutting off the demon's head with lop. "I hate doing this," he disagreed with regret as the head rolled around a bit before taking its last breath.

"It does hurt the human mind. I'd suggest we make like a scared soul and run. The cops could be here any moment and last I checked, you had them consistently up your ass."

"You're right, but who was watching us," he pondered as he walked towards Seans location. "When I got tossed into the air vertically, I saw someone lying in the grass. The light revealed them."

"Shit," Sean thought as he slowly backed away towards the gate.

"There is," the female agreed, causing the man to stop. "They're backing towards the gate, but he's someone we don't need to worry about right now, so let's leave."

"Listen," the man began to raise his voice just enough to be heard across the field. "You have no reason to fear me." His voice was deep and hollow as it echoed.

Sean stopped in his tracks, he realized his breathing was out of control as fear settled in. "Did the female just say she's known I've been here? How?"

Police sirens blared as a cop cruiser whipped around the corner down the street towards the field. They turned around to see that twenty police cars and heavy artillery were on the scene.

"Shit," the man thought as the two jumped over the fence into the night, disappearing.

Sean scattered to his feet and began to run back the way he came, towards the cops. His chest was in pain as he ran and his mind was unable to keep up with his sprinting feet, tripping every other step. The water from the grass flew around his feet, causing him to slide into a fence.

A police car flew past as Sean threw himself into a trashcan to hide, his mind indecisive. "This is absurd," he began to think as he laid low. "First I'm introduced to a man in a mask, and then a spirit?"

Chapter 6

Hell awaits

Sean walked up his apartment complex steps, fumbling around with his keys as he approached his door. His breathing was heavy and his eyes drooped from sleep deprivation. His mind pondered about the night he had just experienced as he unlocked the door. He entered into a lobby with a desk in the middle of the room. He walked towards the elevators that sat to the left of the desk, pressing the "up" button.

It lit up and as he stood there waiting, he heard the female receptionist ask, "There was an incident at your job," she began. "Are you okay?"

Knowing the lady from high school, he answered with an exhausted nod as the elevator doors opened. He entered the elevator, pressing the number 2, letting the elevator take him to his floor as he rose in place. The doors opened, letting Sean step into his hallway.

His phone began to ring in his back pocket as he approached the one hundredth door in the hallway. Sean unlocked his door and entered into his small apartment looking around. Seeing his cats sitting on the couch that was pushed against the wall, he ignored them as he walked past them towards the kitchen where he made a mac and cheese dinner.

The news on the television blared in the background, his name could be heard every now and then as he turned attention towards it.

"Tonight," read a female news anchor. "There was a massive hole crushed into a local Winky Wacky Burgers around ten o' clock. Four suspects appeared to be at the scene, three are currently missing. The fourth man, Adam Dubline, who was a manager at the restaurant, was found dead. It appeared the man ripped himself apart from head to toe, until there was nothing left. Over to you Mackel."

"Such a shame," the anchorman pitied as the camera panned to a man in a blue suit. "In related news, there were some skeletons found disintegrating in a nearby baseball field not too far away from the restaurant. It is believed that these two incidents are related."

A light from the phone he placed on the table next to his plate interrupted the television. He picked it up and saw his girlfriend, Jessica, was calling.

"Hey baby, how's your day been?" he asked nonchalantly.

"Don't pull that shit!" she began barking into the phone. "Where are you at, I've been worried you got killed by a demon or something. Crazy how reality actually got split like that. What do you think would have caused it?" Her voice sounded cheerful as she was always studying paranormal theories, along with space and time theories. "If there were disintegrating bones, it must have been a demon.

Sean was not a big fan of these theories himself though he studied common subjects such as English, Mathematics, and anything that has to do with logic.

"I'm not too familiar with the subject but I can help you come up with some theories," he conversed as he stood up from his chair. He moved the phone from his left ear to his right while he stood up from his seat, walking towards the window that next to the television on the kitchen counter.

"So the news says that there were four people at the restaurant site, but then after that there were also three people seen to have jumped away from a baseball field. Now another media news outlet says that there were two seen at the baseball field, while a third man was seen emerging from the grass. He got away via backyards, it might've been the same way the man went from. They did catch the back of the person's head and I enhanced the image," there was a sudden knock at her door. "Hold on babe, someone's at my door."

"That's weird," Sean began to think. "It's midnight and a half, who would be at her house this late? By the way she phrased that last sentence, she was surprised, so it's not like it's an expected guest." He heard her voice re-emerge back onto the phone, trembling.

"Babe, there's a strange man on my porch," she whispered as fear seeped out of her words.

Sean grabbed his car keys and sprinted out of his door as she begged him for answers on what to do. "Stay inside and don't open the door," he stressed as he ran down his hallway.

He decided not to take the elevator, but to take the stairs since there were only two floors. He shoved the door to the stairwell open before leaping over the railing. He let himself fall to the bottom floor with a loud thump that echoed the halls. He shoved the door open, snapping the hinges as they over stretched. He ran towards his car that sat in the back of his apartment, whipping the door open before jumping into his car and jamming his key into his blue station wagon.

"He's banging on the door, the loud noise is scaring me."

"Babe, I'm on the way. Grab a knife and hide just in case he breaks in."

He sped out of his parking spot over some grass and bushes as he began down the street with the pedal to the floor. When he turned corners, the front of the blue station wagon jammed inwards while the back over slid behind. His truck began to slide as the back tires were unable to keep up. He looked in his rearview mirror to see a cop keeping up with its orange and white lights flashing.

"Shit, it doesn't matter," he thought as he ignored them and pushed the truck even further into another gear. Four more cop cars sped out of alleyways, their sirens blaring as they slipped their cars around corners.

"What the hell," he yelled, clenching the phone hoping Jessica was okay.

The cops behind him began to speak into their microphones.

"Pull over or we will drop spike strips. If you resist further, your car will be demolished by either explosion or fire. An even further resistance will get you a beat down and a one ticket to lifetime in jail. It is advised you pull over before it's too late."

Sean began to shake as fear held his foot on the pedal. "Babe, are you okay?" his voice trembled as he drove.

"Yeah, but he's in my house. I need you babe," she was screaming out of fear. He knew she was small and wasn't able to defend herself.

It felt as if it were forever until Sean arrived at her house with thirty cop cars behind him, his tires blown out and the phone disconnected. News helicopters hovered over them as they observed and recorded everything with large spot lights. Cops stopped their cars to charge Sean, who was charging towards the open door that taunted him. News crews on the ground followed Sean in like a cop on his heels. He ran inside and the strong smell of metal hit his nose immediately.

"JESSICA!" he shouted into the empty house.

He started to run up the stairs to her room as he observed the spilled blood like an overrun bathtub. He looked down the narrow hallway to see a blood trail, it seemed as if the person was assaulted downstairs and ran up here to hide. His heart began to race as he heard a moan from the door at the end of the hallway, causing everything to play in slow motion.

"No, not you. Anybody but you," he thought as he ran down the hall. His heart rushed with every step, causing the blood to splash. His lungs began to give out on him when he approached the locked door, a small moan was heard coming from within. He bashed it in with his shoulder in one blow, seeing his future wife in a pool of her own blood.

"I've been waiting for you," she whispered, leaning against the wall. The moonlight shone in through the dual windows above her head, revealing a small woman with a bump in her stomach wearing glasses.

He rushed towards her and put her head in his hand, she was still breathing as he put his other hand on her soft cheek. Her glasses were broken, and she seemed at peace now. He whispered as he talked and observed her body. There were gashes in her stomach and throat.

"Don't you dare die, come on we had a plan. We had a lot going on for us. You were the only happiness in my life. For eight fucking years, eight!" he shouted as tears poured down his face. He rocked her in his arms as she began to silently talk with what little life she had left.

"I'm sorry baby," she apologized as she gave the most beautiful smile. She gripped his shirt and pulled him closer. "I know this isn't easy but you've gotta forgive those who do harm upon you. It's the only way to true happiness. I love you, and don't worry, we will see each other again." She reassured as her hand loosened, letting go of the grip on his shirt.

He sobbed as he whispered those three words back, rocking her as police busted through the windows and doors to tackle Sean, beating the hell out of him with batons and bats.

The police station was known to harbor many criminals, or people who do stupid things for selfish reasons. There were also kids who were just trying to survive without their parents. Sean sat on the sixth floor, in the four hundred sixty-seventh room. A cold metal chair with arm rests was all that comforted him. His arms were bound to the arms of the chair like some petrifying monster, and his feet were chained to the chair. He stared at the cold metal table as the blood dripped from his face.

An officer walked into the room wearing orange and white with unnecessary sunglasses as he chewed on what seemed to be gum with a smile. He stood six feet and sat down in the metal chair directly in front of Sean.

"So, what's your name?" The officer asked in a genuine tone. He sat with his legs crossed holding a pen and notepad.

Sean sat there in silence as the events from the entire night began to replay in his head over and over. It felt as if Sean were living in an alternate dream world, but he wasn't able to wake up. He just sat there as his heart began to shrink the more and more he soaked in his own pain.

"I understand, you lost your woman…"

"She was seven months pregnant," he argued, hollow-like.

The officer leaned forward in his chair as his legs bent straight, clicking his pen on the table.

"We are doing everything we ca-"

"Fuck you," he spat as he weakly raised his head. "You're going to blame the murder on me, aren't you?"

The smile began to fade away from the cop's face as he sat back.

"You're a smart man because that is true. You did however, make us chase you to her house and by the time anybody got there, she was bloody in your arms."

Sean began to get angry with every word that seeped from the cops mouth.

"You cowards come in many," he complained as he began to clench his fists. "Those many cowards die so easily because they rely on each other to keep them alive, but what happens when the man runs out of allies? Do you think he's going to fight or run? I'll tell you, run, because they know that the allies who died wouldn't even know they ran. Cowards, all of you," he began to stand up until the chains kept him bound to the chair.

"A skinny man like you can't break those chains, which a restraint like this is perfect for you. About five units of cops were chasing you for twenty miles, why?"

A sudden silence filled the room as he sat there, letting anger and sadness circulate through his veins as he began to care less and less for his morals.

"Have you ever heard of adrenaline?" he suddenly asked.

Sean burst out of the chair ad the sound of chains snapping was heard throughout the building. The officer flew backwards out of his chair, surprised that Sean was able to break the chains.

He flipped the table as the officer jumped back onto his feet with his gun in hand. Eight shots rang out as they collided with the metal table that was now rushing towards him. It sent him crashing into a wall, squishing him as Sean made a straight line to the door. He grabbed the handle and ripped the heavy thick steel from its' hinges.

Outside of the room, officers looked in pure shock as Sean ran to the right, towards the stairs. Every officer pulled out their guns and began to fire at the man who disappeared behind the staircase door.

"After him," one of the officers yelled and pointed.

In a rush, they all began to storm the stairwell with guns in hand.

"Where did he go?" one asked as another pointed upwards saying,

"There he is," as Sean was seen running up the stairs towards the rooftop.

The officers stormed up the stairs to the roof where Sean was holding a full automatic rifle.

"Stand back or I will shoot," he warned as he backed closer and closer towards the edge that was fifty feet away.

"You don't have to do this," a man in white bargained as he pushed himself towards the front of the crowd. His bushy mustache nearly covered his entire face. "Listen, we understand you lost your girlfriend and child. We also understand as to why you would kill them, so just put down the gun and end this peacefully. If you do keep holding that gun however, you will be shot on site. You don't want your family to see you with holes, do you?" He raised his hand as a signal to his cops.

"Fuck you! Do none of you even realize the reality of this situation?" Tears began to flow like a river from Seans eyes. "I was speeding so I could make it to her in time, so that I didn't have to witness what I just saw. I watched as the blood from the gashes in her stomach poured from her mouth. She wasn't just bleeding for herself, she was bleeding for both of them you sacks of shit!" Sean yelled as he emptied a clip into their frontline, killing all that stood there. The second line responded by becoming the front line.

Shots were heard ringing out and lines of bullets began to approach Sean, whose arms were raised in surrender. The gun he held was on the ground empty, and his eyes closed as if he were going to sleep.

A man and a woman appeared from thin air, carrying riot shields tight to their chest as bullets began to ricochet. He opened his eyes in disbelief.

"Who are you guys?" Sean asked as they protected him, the shields now pressed against their shoulders as the second round of bullets rang out.

The man had a sword on the right of his hip and spoke louder than the bullets.

"We gotta go, if we don't we're all dead," he ushered as the bullets stopped cracking their shield. "They've gotta reload," he informed as the front line men emptied their guns.

"Let's go," he commanded as he grabbed Sean by the arm.

"Where are we going?" he asked as the man dragged him to the end of the roof.

"Dispatch, we have a twelve-fifty six. Bring them out," they heard an officer say as they fled.

"We're taking the next platform," the man bantered as they leaped off of the rooftop, crashing onto another one slightly lower. "Let's go," he ordered as they began to skip rooftops.

Cops in helicopters and tanks were heard moving in on their position not too far away as they leaped through the large city.

"They're gonna get us," Sean panicked as they approached a gap too wide to jump across.

They stopped and looked in between the gap, seeing that the drop and jump was too grave. They stood in a triangle as the man in black looked at the woman in pink.

"No they're not, Scarlett, get to that rooftop," the man directed to the woman in all pink.

She nodded and began back up to the beginning end of the rooftop and turned around. She sprinted with her arms folded and her legs barely visible before reaching the gap, jumping and clearing the width of the gap. She rolled into a crouching position then looked up to give the signal with a thumbs up.

"What was that?" Sean asked as tanks began to surround the tall buildings they stood on.

"A signal," the man reassured as he gripped Sean by the right arm with both hands. He began to swing him around and around, making Sean feel nauseous as he let him go.

He began to spin in the air like a thrown baton, the female had her hands out to catch him with force that tossed her backwards. Helicopters were above their heads as the tanks pointed at the base of the buildings they stood on, and the ones around those.

"We are fucked," Sean panicked as he got up rubbing his head.

"There is no further resistance here," the helicopter with a microphone instructed. "Either you give up now or die due to the collapse of the building, or we could kill you outright. We have twelve tanks in total, four at the base of each building you can jump onto and the one you currently stand on. Either take a plummet or give in silently." The microphone shut off as everything became still.

"Make us!" the man shouted.

The microphone turned back on, "FIRE!" it screamed.

The helicopter blades stopped spinning as the birds stopped in mid flight and the bullets from the helicopter began to reach the trio.

"Scarlette, plan B!" the man yelled as time began again, sending bullets raining onto the rooftop he was standing on.

Simultaneously, Scarlette nodded and turned around, swiping at the air in front of her as a black and white tiny dotted portal appeared. While she dodged a hail storm of bullets, she ran towards Sean, who was cowering under a billboard. She grabbed him by the collar and ran back towards her portal before jumping into it. They disappeared as the buildings collapsed from the tanks blowing out their bases. The man ran and jumped onto the side of the building that collided into the one he stood on, sliding down its side as a helicopter shot at him.

The glass began to break underneath his body as began to understand that he was out of options. He stomped his foot on a cracked window he saw beneath him, causing him to slide into the hole. He cut himself on shards all the way down.

With the building still falling, the man recovered with his hand gripping the ceiling. He steadied himself to his feet and began to run up the ninety degree angle to the open window as detached his sword's handle, revealing a grappling hook. He clicked the button, throwing out the hook that caught onto something.

 He let himself hang onto the rope while he swiftly let the building fall beneath him, causing a mass cloud of debris and dust.

Hanging onto his rope, he swung from the helicopter as it began to tilt and swerve, trying to throw the man. The helicopter smashed itself into a building across the street, causing his body to smash into the glass. His ribs ached from the pain and his arms felt like they were tearing. He looked down to see that the tanks had machine guns along with an army behind it pointing at him.

"Well shit," he thought as he looked up and began to swing himself from side to side.

Making it shake, he began to gain momentum as he swung wider and wider in the air before launching himself into the seating of the helicopter. He looked up to see three men towering over him as he lay on his back, throwing down police swords into the ground as he dodged. He stood up and began to fight the three men in the seating area. He ducked under all three punches, making them punch each other. Two of them pulled out their knives and swung at him while the third sat in one of the chairs. He sidestepped and grabbed both of their arms, pulling them together.

Their heads collided, causing the helicopter to lose balance. The two men fell to their deaths as the third man stood from his seat. Giving him a glare, he planted his foot into the man's chest, causing him to plummet out of the spinning helicopter to the ground below.

He made the helicopter steady with his feet as he began to make his way to the seat of the helicopter where the driver and passenger had already jumped out.

"Wait, if they had ejector seats," he pondered as the helicopter beeped loudly and spun out of control. "Great," he bantered sarcastically as he grabbed the controls.

He put a foot on the dashboard and grabbed the wheel with two hands. He prayed for dear life as the whipping of the chopper began to snap his bones.

Yanking at the steering wheel, he managed to stabilize the helicopter and pull it upwards, slimly missing a tank. It was only just enough for it to be tipsy, but still usable and smoky. The tanks began to shoot their missiles towards the tipsy helicopter within twenty feet. They missed the helicopter slightly as he began to try and gain altitude.

The vehicle began to light afire, causing it to sputter out of control and make a nose dive downwards towards the army below. He jumped from the helicopter, ready to meet his fate when a sudden black field of energy appeared underneath his feet, swallowing him.

He fell to the ground with a thump as the room he was in was dark and empty.

"What the hell?" he asked as a light turned on to reveal a singular desk.

The desk had an overwhelming amount of papers and rotten apples that littered the wood. The room stank and the wall behind the turned around chair was covered in a red liquid.

"Is that blood?" he thought as the chair began to slowly spin around.

A muscular man filled the chair, his hair was blonde and his eyes were blue. He had a very defined jawline along with very, very, very, large shoulders. This man was huge, standing at seven foot eight. He stood up and began to walk towards the tiny man wearing a mask while holding a large orang3 cat in his arms, petting it from its head to its tail.

"My name is Principle Scorch, how are you doing?" he introduced as they stood mere inches from each other.

Chapter 7

Byron's beginning

"I can't believe we were able to get tickets for this concert," a man wearing jeans and an "Amy Kindell" T-shirt with her face on the front, said. He stood five foot eight, and his hair stood on his head like a neatly trimmed bush. A man five foot seven walked beside the slightly taller guy in the middle of a crowd.

"I know, this is awesome. People say that guys who listen to her are weird, but they don't even know she sings behind electronic music." The crowd began to dissipate after they entered the parking lot to smoke before the show.

"Hey Byron," the man in the T-shirt uttered.

"Yeah what's up," he responded as he looked up from looking for his lighter. He had an unlit cigarette in his mouth.

A woman in a sparkly green shirt and black jeans, approached the two. Her heels made her two feet taller as they clicked against the cement. She wore a microphone over her mouth and glasses across her blue eyes.

"Do you two know who I am?" she asked as her voice squeaked.

"Yeah, you're Mrs. Amy. Aren't you supposed to be backstage or something?" he asked as he lit his cigarette, taking a puff and releasing it.

"Dude, you're not that cool," his friend responded with an eye roll.

"I'm not here to argue, but I am here to ask you both to come backstage with me. I was picking out two random people to be on the stage with me. I don't like to be up there alone, men like to climb the stage," She lectured as she pulled out two tickets and badges from her back pocket and awkwardly shoved them towards the two.

"I've heard of that, but don't you have bodyguards?" Byron asked.

She deeply inhaled through her nose and out of her mouth loudly.

"Unfortunately they died on the way here, there's someone who's been chasing us since we left the hotel. They say that it's just fans, but they're too aggressive to be just fans, you know?"

"Sounds like you definitely need us," the other guy spoke in confidence as he took the passes and badges.

"So, what's your guys' name?" she asked as she motioned to leave.

"I'm Byron, and this is Chuck. We were coming to see the show, but I guess we can help you stay alive." Squishing his cigarette bud against the wall, Byron took his pass and began to follow the woman to the staging area.

He noticed there were a lot of people, it was going to be easy to get lost in this place. He looked around and kept a mental note on the female. There were so many people that it was overwhelming, how was he supposed to know the difference?

"If you're wondering who to look for," she turned her head to say, her voice more serious than before. "They're men who wear orange caps, not policemen, so if you kill any, that's on you." She informed.

They walked to an elevator in the garage where Amy pressed the up arrow, causing it to light up.

"We're going to a restaurant. This building isn't nearly as big as the school, so it's going to be easier to navigate," she clicked her heels against the ground as the elevator doors opened.

They entered the elevator one at a time, with Amy to be the last to enter. She pressed the number three on the number pad, making the elevator shake before elevating. The doors opened after a few short seconds before they walked into a waiting room where a waitress stood at the greeting desk.

"Hi Mrs. Amy, are these your plus two?" the lady asked.

"Yeah, are you sure there's nobody else here?" she replied.

Byron and Chuck stood there awkwardly as they began to lean into each other and whisper.

"So this is a restaurant," Chuck began. "Why aren't we going to the concert on the first floor?"

"I don't know, but something isn't right. She told us that her bodyguards were killed this morning, but how was she able to escape without dying herself?" Byron asked.

"Hm, a very good question," he replied.

The waiter and Amy turned around to Byron and Chuck, signaling them to follow. They were led through a very small dining area into a small kitchen with no employees. Chuck began to worry as he saw a handgun swinging from the woman's belt.

They were taken through a door in the back of the kitchen that revealed a humongous lobby, the type of lobby you'd see in museums.

"This is huge," Byron and Chuck synchronized as they looked up and around in awe.

"Come on," Amy ushered politely as they stood in front of an open door to the left.

They stopped glancing around and walked through the door, revealing a narrow hallway with many doors. They were then led down the hall to the first left as they turned to continue walking further in. At the fifth door, three zero five, the waitress opened the door and stood aside. They proceeded to walk through and as soon as they were inside, the waitress closed the door shut.

The three began to walk down past bathroom stalls and sinks towards a purple tent in the corner. Amy approached it and opened the curtain, allowing them to enter the cold and comfortable area as they gathered onto a circle bench with a table in the middle.

"This problem is bigger than any of us and I have a direct line of contact to the High Priest," Amy lectured as they began to settle into the bench.

"The High Priest?" Byron asked.

"You are going to need to know this, but your friend Chuck can't be here, but he'll be fine." She assured, clicking a button under the table that caused the wall behind Chuck to open as the bench threw him into a dark pit.

"Why?" he echoed as he fell.

"You can't do that," Byron argued as he was about to get up before getting shoved down with just one finger

"I'm not just a singer Byron, I'm the High Priests' Mistress. I was sent here to give you information because there was no other way to tell you. Killing off your family would seem ineffective and you don't really care about your friends. I have access to you and all of the brothers that you were separated from."

"Why're you here?" he asked angrily.

"That's why I'm here, to tell you why I'm here. Now, there is a man that goes by the name 'Principle Scorch'. He's been under the radar from police to yearly building inspections. The man fled here after he had his own omni-verse erased…"

"What's an omni-verse," he interrupted.

She sighed and dropped her head.

"I guess I have to explain this to you now." she looked up at his face filled with wonder. "So basically the solar system we are standing in is actually a galaxy that has a mirror galaxy that mimics closely to ours. If you don't understand that then imagine this, the current embodiment of you is an idiot, while the embodiment of you in the mirror universe is completely smart and knew all of this already. The galaxy and the mirror galaxy combined make a universe, and a group of more than one of these universes makes a multiverse, which henceforth makes an omni-verse.

"Makes sense, so how is this single man going to destroy an entire omni-verse?" Byron asked as he sat up, putting his wrists on his knees and folding his hands.

"There's no easy way to say this but, an all out invasion. To be put in the plainest, when he came to this universe he dropped all of the magic and ki he used to have. It's because when certain beings travel through the omni-verses, they drop all of their abilities from the previous omni-verse to gain the natural abilities of the omni-verse they would then currently stand in."

"So, what you're saying is that this man can hop dimensions?"

"Let me speak," she silenced him as she put her finger up. "Scorch is able to hop dimensions, it's how he got to this universe. Back to the problem at hand, he created a serum where when injected into the ground, the injector can control an entire population of people telepathically. It gets crazier, he also made a second serum where if injected into the ground, it could revive anything that was buried."

Byron sat in shock as his mind was unable to process what she just explained.

"Wait, no, that means…" he stammered.

"It means that not only is the dead going to rise, humans are going to be controlled and fed to the undead, leaving no survivors. The worst part is that he's been sending minions after me, and they've killed my entire crew. He's also been looking for a man who lives in this universe."

Amy began to reach under her seat, fumbling around for what seemed like forever until she pulled out an assault rifle. Byron nervously chuckled as his smile began to fade.

"Yeah it's about to get ugly, and I need you to help," she warned as she pulled out a second one, handing him the other one.

"I don't…" Byron began to say before he began to think. "There's no way what father taught could be true, does it all lead to killing?" he thought.

"Nobody said you have to shoot anyone, just shoot *at* them if you want."

A loud boom was heard as smoke filled the bathroom and a flashbang rolled in, blinding them both. She opened the curtain and began to spray at the door, killing five men in great dane masks.

"We've gotta go," she commanded as she looked at Byron then back at the cleared entrance as her hair flipped.

With confidence, Byron bursted out through the curtain with the rifle scope pressed up to his cheek. He began to tactically shoot enemies that came through the bathroom door. They began to spill into the hallway where there were more men in masks. There was a man heard from the first floor on the stage giving an announcement that the show was being canceled, but also told everybody that they should remain in the gathering area.

They began to shoot at their enemies that filled the narrow hallway as more men showed up around the corner at the end of the hall, only to meet their doom. They looked at each other when their guns clicked, notifying that they were out of ammunition.

"Are you out of ammo?" Byron yelled to Amy behind a segment of a wall for cover.

"Yea, but here's a knife," Amy suggested as she tossed a combat knife sideways.

He caught it with his open palm, gripping the handle in his fist with the blade pointing to his right as he left cover.

"What's the layout?" Byron asked as they gathered in the middle of the hallway.

"It's not a big building," she reminded him as they began to run down the narrow hallway. They zipped past doors and stabbed men as they appeared. They took the right turn and ran through the door at the end of that hall, "We have to go across this lobby to the waiting room, then we can leave through the elevator.

"I never thought they'd do an indoor concert, this place is huge."

"They're not, we just came up here to look down at the concert after our talk, but plans always change," she puffed through breaths as they ran through the dining room door into the kitchen.

While he ran, Byron saw a knife appear from the corner of a wall, which almost cut him as he bent backwards immediately. He then grabbed the man by his arm and tossed him into their partner across the counter to his right. They looked at the door to the waiting room, realizing that enemies were pouring inside and soon they were surrounded.

They began to dodge and kick as their enemies tried to put the two down with nothing but their bare hands. Smoke filled the room as Amy felt her arm getting tugged and as she did, she grabbed Byron's arm, dragging them both into the waiting room. The waitress was sitting there smiling nervously with her gun shaking in her left hand.

"Hey, so you might have to leave," she proposed nicely as she stood to escort the two out.

"Yeah, when the smoke clears, they'll know we're gone. Thank you for everything," she praised the waitress. "Towards the elevator," she told Byron as they began to sprint through the open dual door.

It seemed as if it were forever before they were on the garage floor, when the doors opened, tons and tons of "minion" cars covered the garage.

"We need backup," she talked into her mic.

Suddenly one car set aflame, causing it to blow up and create a domino effect of exploding cars. Torn bodies flew into the air as the glass and doors flew off. The entire garage was littered with fire and bodies when the smoke cleared. They began to make their way to the exit, where a car would take them to a helicopter.

"Listen," she began as they climbed into the back of a taxi. "We have to meet up with three other people you need to know. These three will be by your side for the rest of your life, and no, you won't like them."

Amy turned around and saw three cars on the street tailing them, dodging cars as they sped down the street.

"Driver, a bit faster and more reckless please?" she asked as she pulled a radio from under the seat. "Your three allies have these, make sure to use them to communicate."

The driver tipped his hat as the taxi began to increase in speed, causing the three to press up against their seat as the driver dodged and weaved through the heavy traffic. They grabbed onto the handlebars attached to the ceiling as the car began to lose balance. They turned down alleyways to make their way back onto main streets.

"Bison, do you read?" Amy asked into her ear radio.

Static was heard over the radio as a voice came to life.

"Yeah, what's your current situation?" A man with a serious tone questioned.

"We're almost there," Amy informed as they approached a tall building with a helicopter atop.

"Shit," Byron swore as he looked out of the passenger window. He saw a man not too far ahead, on one of the buildings, holding what seemed to be some sort of launcher. "ROCKET!" Byron yelled as he covered himself.

A missile was seen to be diving towards the taxi at maximum speed, hitting the hood with an insane explosion. The car flipped as it set aflame and the tires popped. The glass shattered as the two rolled around on the ceiling of the taxi, forgetting their seatbelts.

Men began to approach the car with their rifles and their fingers steady on the trigger when suddenly the men were enveloped in a thick white smog. They began to fall one by one as a man in a red gas mask appeared to be slitting throats, along with another man, in a blue gas mask, and a woman in a black gas mask with a pink backpack. They began to approach the flaming car while the white smog dissipated, and began to rip the doors from the hinges. Pulling the two from the wreckage, they began to lift them onto their shoulders.

"Get to that building," the man in the red gas mask muffled.

"Don't you mean, get to that chopper?" the man in the blue gas mask bantered.

"Not the time," he silenced as they jogged down the street towards the building.

Military appeared on the scene, fighting off every man that appeared on the scene. They dodged bullets as they passed and began to get closer and closer, they couldn't run much longer.

"I'm going to hold them off," the man in blue muffled as the other two kept running with Byron and Amy on their shoulders. He took his fully automatic rifle off of his back and began to unload into the men that were behind them. He killed about thirty in one clip.

"Good training," the man in red congratulated as they jogged towards the tanks that stood in front of the radio building.

At the same time, the man and the woman picked up the two and cradled them in their arms, sprinting at full speed. As they were approaching the building, the man in reds' radio began to spit static.

"I'm down," the man in blue coughed into his radio.

He turned around to see his ally lying in the middle of an absolute beatdown, they were beating him with bats and kicking him harshly. They began to spit and curse, causing anger to surge through the man in red as he charged even faster towards the building.

As they entered the building, passing tanks on the way, they put the two on the floor before collapsing themselves. The cool air hit their sweaty bodies immediately, sending chills down their spines. The male and female were currently unconscious and bleeding from the head.

"This isn't good," the man in red thought as he turned around and rushed back outside with anger surging through his veins. "Don't forget, stay calm and remain attentive."

He shoved past the military that tried to hold him back, rushing towards the now mushy man. He pulled the sword from his waist as he jumped towards the center. He spun in a circle with one hand on his sword, slicing everyone in the radius. He landed next to the man as he observed his surroundings, it seemed as if there were armies behind them. He put his ally on his shoulder and began to run towards the building as a bullet whipped by his eye. He turned his attention behind himself to see an enemy tank with a machine gun.

Starting to sprint faster, he crashed through the front line of officers that almost shot him dead and entered into the building.

"Can we evacuate?" he asked as he put the man against the wall next to the other two injured.

"You're injured," she warned as she watched him fall to the ground.

"When did I…" he pondered as he fell.

She ran to his side as he closed his eyes, pulling her pink bag from her back and unzipping it. She began pulling out a first aid kit, opening it to reveal bandages, alcohol, string, and a needle. Among and along with the few items, she pulled out a small pair of scissors and began to cut Paul's shirt off. Ripping it open, she began to recite a personal list she made.

"If they can't breathe, check their lungs, and if they have bullet holes," she mumbled as she pulled out tweezers and alcohol. "Take out the bullet and sterilize the wound."

She put the tweezers to the seal on the tip of the rubbing alcohol bottle and broke it, placing it aside. She pressed the tweezers inside of a wound on the man's neck, squeezing and pulling a medium assault bullet from the wound and dropped it on the ground. She repeated the process on the right portion of his back, his stomach, and the back of his left leg.

Amy and Byron began to regain consciousness as the female was finishing the last wound.

"What the hell," Amy grunted as she sat up.

"The three of us had to save your sorry asses," the woman barked as she put alcohol on a cloth, "This might hurt," she softly assured the man as she patted his head.

Dapping it onto the barely conscious man's wound, he began to fill the building from top to bottom with his howl.

"What happened," the man in blue asked as he regained consciousness.

"There was a hail fire of bullets when this guy saved you from your death," she snarled.

"So you're telling me I didn't get shot?" The man in blue asked the woman in black.

"They surrounded you, but now isn't the time because we've gotta get upstairs," the woman in black responded as she put the now bandaged man on her shoulder.

She began to run up the stairs as the others recovered and followed behind. They climbed floor after floor as their legs burned like calories.

"How many floors are in this building?" the man in blue asked.

"Fifty floors," the woman commanded confidently, striding onwards. "You guys are weak, we're only on floor twenty," she taunted as she began to sprint up the stairs, skipping every other step.

"We gotta keep up," Byron proposed as he began to sprint up the stairs.

Amy and the man in the blue mask followed behind the others, reaching the rooftop with hardly any time wasted. The helicopter sat there hovering as the blades whipped the air around. The pilot stood in front of the driver door and as they approached, he spoke.

"Are you guys ready to leave?"

With a deadly glare, the woman holding the man climbed aboard without saying a word when suddenly the ground began to shake.

"It's starting," Amy warned as she climbed on and sat down.

"Come on Byron," the man in blue yelled as he reached his arm out.

"I cannot," Byron blindly disagreed.

"What? Come on, the building could collapse," the man in blue tried to plead.

Byron began to climb aboard the helicopter when the building suddenly shifted, causing it to crack and crumble underneath them.

Byron lost his grip on the helicopter and slipped back onto the falling building. The female looked down at the street to see the ground breaking upwards, revealing dead people rising from their graves. Every civilian they saw was soon walking themselves into the hands of undead. There were so many, it's as if it was meant to revive dead skeletons as well.

As they began to shake, the helicopter lifted off, leaving Byron falling with the building. Regaining consciousness, the man in red realized the situation at hand immediately. He got up and as his allies held him off, he yelled for Byron, reaching his arm out of the helicopter.

"I'm going for him," he challenged as he ripped their arms away and began to free fall to the dead below.

"Bison!" the female yelled.

Chapter 8

Where it all began

Paul awoke in a small dim room lying in a queen sized bed. He looked around to see his bed next to the wall and a bed next to his. At the bottom of the bed, Gwen sat in a chair in front of a desk with a mirror.

"Oh," Gwen spoke, surprised as she turned around to look at Paul. "You're awake, good. I have information on the principle of Skylark…"

"What're you talking about?" Paul rudely interrupted as he sat up, rubbing his head.

"You whispered that you might have to create the multiverse warriors to protect the omni-verses from any evil," she began again as she stood up from her chair and walked to his bedside. "You've already shown you're worthy, just embrace your inner twin."

"Multiverse Warriors? Inner twin?" he began to mumble.

"Well, I made up the entire Multiverse Warriors name for your future group. You're going to be a great leader in battle," she exclaimed as she sat down at the end of his bed, crossing her legs.

"I don't want to lead, I would rather have somebody else lead."

"It would be better for someone else to be the leader, you're too feisty. Oh and I got rid of your Lucyfer problem. I blew her house away," she yelped with excitement.

"What!" he yelled. "I wanted to get out but I didn't want them blown up."

"I already went through your memories, the ones from this life and the past life. You're a really good guy."

"I didn't want you to go through my memories either," he argued as he rubbed his head, trying to think of anything that might have been erased.

"Don't worry, I didn't erase any memories, I just emplanted a," she stopped talking and closed her eyes.

"A highly microscopic telepathic radio. I made it myself, only for you," she thought into his mind.

"That's so creepy," he thought as his head tingled. "That still doesn't get you off the hook. Blowing up houses and killing innocents is wrong."

"You call those people innocent," she snipped, shooting him a death glare from the foot of the bed. She planted her hands onto the end of the bed as she stood up with pride in her voice.

"All she did was turn you against your brother and then treated you like him when you didn't comply with her orders. She made you tell lies to people that could have actually helped because you were afraid that she was going to what? Choke or throw a few knives at you. She put you and your brother out on the winter streets multiple times, and for what? To punish and send a message, her mind is twisted and I'm glad she lives in hell."

There was a sudden silence that lingered in the room as the two stared away from each other.

"Ahem," he cleared his throat. "Well, since you put it that way," he agreed as he reached for the water to the right of his bed on the night table.

"Don't drink that," she cautioned as she took the cup from him before it touched his mouth. "It's a mix of alcohol and some substances I snuck from the underworld to make an arm restoration potion."

"How did you do that?" He thought in shock as Gwen suddenly appeared next to him

"Well, as I mentioned before, I used to abuse my body so that I could learn how to heal it, just because I was bored."

She sat the cup down onto the bedside table before continuing her important message.

"We need to first find Sean since you don't want to be a leader, he's the more logical one between you three. I'm obviously the medic, your brother Byron will be the normal guy nobody likes, and you will be the man who helps those in need, and only those in need. We do not involve ourselves into other peoples problems unless solidified by information on who is wrong."

"Sounds good to me," he concurred as he swung his legs to the bedside. "Where do we get started?" He asked as he put on his black jeans and a solid red shirt.

"Well as I've mentioned before, we need to find the leader Sean. I don't know anything about him because he's your brother," she blushed as she watched Paul dress.

"Can you please elaborate? Why do you know so much about me?"

"Does that really matter?" Gwen asked as she returned to the end of the bed.

"I mean, you are going to stick by my side from here on out, right?" Paul questioned as he stood to his feet.

As Gwen sat on the bed, she gave a slight sigh before answering his question.

"When I was younger, I overheard my dad holding a conversation with The Creator. They talked about who's soul he shouldn't touch since it does hold a tiny secret."

"Weird," he pondered as he sat next to Gwen and grabbed his boot from the bottom of the bed.

"Is it really?" she questioned, cocking her head to the side.

She stood up and walked to the dresser she was occupying, brushing off the conversation. She opened up the top drawer, revealing four masks. A red one, a blue one, a black one, and a purple one all lined up. She picked up the red and black mask along with a pink bookbag that sat on the floor next to the dresser.

"You'll wear the red one, since it is your favorite color. You do like wearing masks, right?" she asked as she handed him the mask.

"It's actually really cool. If I had a sword, that'd be kickass," he chippered as he put his mask on.

"I mean, you are going to be a warrior," she responded as she walked towards the dual door closet, opening it as Paul's eyes glistened with excitement. She knelt down and picked up an object that sat next to her spare bookbag. She then crouched and squirmed further into the closet, rummaging around through items.

"So, where did you get all of this?" Paul asked as he patiently waited.

He observed some of the objects in the room, such as a pair of swords behind a shield hanging on the wall behind the beds. He also saw a painting of a painfully beautiful sunset hanging on the wall above her dresser. He also noticed a few gems and books with symbols scattered around in the closet.

"I built all of it myself from the forests unoccupied by humans. There are actually three islands on this Earth, not just two. It's also known that the third island has some animals I've never seen. There were a ton of lurking animals that walked on all fours, birds bigger than me flew around in the skies. Anyway," she finished as she backed out of the closet.

"I found some rare minerals and rocks to create the perfect invulnerable weapon. No matter how much you bend it, slam it, this sucker isn't breaking. Hell, you could shoot an assault rifle at it, point blank range and the only thing you'll end up doing is eating metal," she explained as she presented a long object under a sheet in her upwards open palms. It sat upon a brown baldric as she held it up towards Paul and kneeled,

"I now pronounce you Bison, the second hand in the Multiverse Warriors."

He chuckled as he approached her and picked up the sword, "You're really into this aren't you?" he asked as he uncovered the object, revealing a red and brown scabbard. "That is badass," he chippered as he grinned. "You have been reading my mind."

"Well yeah, I kind of had nothing else to do but study medicine and medieval war stuff like potions and witch craft. I've learned to reverse spells and most kinds of healing spells."

"You're broken," he bragged as he put the baldric around his waist, there was a single loop on the side for the sword.

"Yeah," she smiled. "I do wanna be the perfect wife one day."

He blushed and uncovered the sword, revealing a narrow blade that slanted inwards at the top to make the tip.

"Holy hell, this is single wielded," he began to slice and dice the air. "Can I be honest?" he asked as his smile began to fade.

"You can't hide anything but sure."

"That's scary," he responded. "I honestly have no idea what I'm doing."

"I know," she agreed as she stood up. "I learned everything that you need to know about fighting and swords. I also have certain skills of my own, so if you need help, I'll be there."

There was a sudden knock at the door, banging three times as the voice from beyond the wall yelled, "Police, open up."

Gwen grabbed her pink bookbag and stood up, "We gotta go," she instructed, grabbing Paul's arm.

Putting the sword through the knot, Paul was dragged to the window next to the bed where Gwen was lifting it open. A fire escape leading to the narrow alley below was revealed from behind the black paper on the window. It was nearly dark, around eight o'clock.

"We can use this as an escape," she informed as she climbed outside.

The person at the door began knocking harder and louder, making the door puff in with every blow. Paul followed Gwen onto the metal, shaky gate like staircase.

"This seems safe," he sarcastically snarked as Gwen closed the window. "Do you mind telling me what's going on?" he asked as they ran down the steps, looking down to the narrow street below.

"You don't remember, do you?" she asked as they ran down the shaky stairwell. "Satin has had demons chasing you down since the day you left hell. Follow my lead," she finished as she pressed herself against the railing to look down. "That's twelve floors, if we fall we die."

She looked across of the street to see another fire escape and climbed onto the railing, preparing herself for a scary jump.

"We are not," he disagreed as she prepared her footing and bit her tongue.

"Either let that thing catch you," she announced bravely as she leaped from the fire escape, reaching her arm out and catching the railing three floors below. "Or jump and live through an adrenaline rush," she yelled from below.

"This is crazy," Paul thought as he looked at the human demon above him to Gwen before regrettably climbing onto the railing.

He prepared his footing the best he could and leaped with his arms sprawled out. Jumping down five floors, he barely caught onto the railing.

"Shit," she worried as she watched him pass her. "If you do that again, it might break your arm. Try not to aim so low, remember, it's not about the distance, it's about the safety." She began to jump down three floors at a time until she landed onto the ground.

Looking above, the demon began to get angry as Paul recovered to attempt another jump. He climbed himself up onto the railing, leaping three floors down and catching the railing. As soon as he was safe, the demon purposely jumped and caused the cautious staircase to collapse. It hung onto a flag outside of someone's window as it watched Paul and the staircase freefall.

The stairwell began to tumble as Paul began to feel himself freefall as he heard Gwen from the street below.

"Jump!" Gwen yelled.

Paul recovered, planting both of his feet into a crouching position onto the side of the stairwell. He jumped to the stairwell next to it, falling about six floors down. He looked down at the street just below as his adrenaline surged through his veins. He let himself fall onto the ground, landing on both feet.

"That was intense," she congratulated as they ran out of the alleyway into the crowd.

"Where are we going?" Paul asked as they ran down the sidewalk, shoving past the thick crowd.

The traffic was light and the sun was beginning to set. Around this time, people began to walk to their favorite restaurants and stores since gas prices began to rocket.

"We're going somewhere open," she explained as they almost fell around corners. "Remember, we are protectors but we don't put innocent civilians in the way. Civilians that enact on anything sinful can be treated in any way. For example, if there is a town actively supporting a cult, like praying to them, then the entire town should suffer."

"So what's your current reli…"

"There is none of that here, ever. There is just the truth, okay?" She badgered as they ran through an alley in between the school.

This alley was very popular for the football team of Skylark as it led to the football field.

"We'll fight it here," she panted as she ran, stopping in the middle of the field at the zero and turning around.

A man in a brown trenchcoat wearing sunglasses began to approach them. He stood approximately six feet and had a clean face. He began to talk and his voice was deep.

"You two seem to be doing fine," the demon taunted as he approached from the alley.

Paul put Gwen behind himself and a hand on his sword as the man crept closer and closer towards the frightened two.

"There's no need for that Paul, I'm just here as a nice checkup from her father."

"You want us dead," Paul confronted as he gripped his sword's handle.

"First," her voice began in his head as she stood pressed to his back. "You need to size the man up, use your martial arts and boxing to understand how he moves. Then, when the chance gives itself, attack with your sword."

"Right," he whispered, letting go of the handle.

The man raised his arms and revealed two green objects inside of his hands. He threw them towards the two, causing Paul to turn around and pick up Gwen. He ran from the near death explosion towards a bench not too far away. The man began to throw more and more green grenades, making craters all throughout the field.

He threw Gwen onto the bench, causing her to almost fall onto her back as he ran in a wide circle around the man. He began to run straight and charge the man, throwing his right fist with fury.

The man responded by dodging, causing his fist to fly past his face. He grabbed Paul's arm and punched him in the face, then kicked him in the gut. He then threw him across the field, making him roll into the goal post.

Paul looked up, still dazed from the impact, to see twelve grenades flying towards him. He stood to his feet and ran to the right and into the out of bounds, circling to the man in the trenchcoat. He jumped and spun himself and kicked the demon in the face, knocking his glasses off.

The man looked up and stared at Paul in the eyes. Paul realized that where the man's eyes were supposed to be was filled with nothing but darkness. The man lifted his long arm and let it fall limply downwards, crashing into the ground as Paul leaped the left out of the way.

The being swung his arm once again sideways, right under Paul, who jumped over it and threw himself towards the being. He landed a punch into the man's chest, causing it to stumble a bit as the blow took its air from its lungs.

"Damn," Gwen cheered. "You know how to punch," she yelled from the bench.

He jumped upwards towards the enemy's face, meeting him eye to eye. His soul immediately wanted to run and hide as he punched him three times in the face.

Paul landed back onto his feet as the man lifted an unpinned grenade to his chest. It blew up and he was sent flying backwards as he clutched his left eye.

"Grr raa," he began as he kneeled on the ground trying to control himself.

"Hm?" the being wondered as he tilted his head.

Seeing Paul clutching his eye, Gwen realized that neither of his eyes were busted. "What's going on?" she wondered as she closed her eyes to enter his head.

She opened her eyes to being surrounded by a large and noisy crowd. Gwen did her best to look up and around to see where she was, and she instantly knew that this was a humongous medieval battle coliseum.

"It's a medieval battle coliseum, but why?" she pondered as she looked down to see what seemed like Paul and a second Paul flinging blood from each other as they fought.

"That must be his twin," she thought as she raced down the steps towards the exit. "And this must be his imagination where he fights all of his inner fears. It seems as if this one is winning, but why?" she asked herself as she wandered around into an empty area.

"Why is he fighting his twin?" she thought as she noticed something to her left. She began to run towards the gated entrance to the battlefield without realizing it was the battlefield.

Gwen peered in through the gate, listening to the conversation.

"You don't know what it's like to hate these people, they're all mad. Kill them all now and get it over with," the barely injured Paul bargained.

"You're not me, I don't kill. There's no need, humanity is innocent," argued the bloody and weak Paul on his knees.

Paul two walked towards the original Paul, grabbing him by the shirt and lifting him up to look him in the bloody eyes.

"You're weak, do you even know who I am? Huh!" he exclaimed as he put a blow into his gut.

"You're just a figment of my imagination," he coughed as he fell to the ground.

"All of those teachings from those so-called churches, you gained me. I am nothing more than a reasonable ally. I am your angelic twin and humanity needs to burn."

"So that's his twin," she whispered, immediately closing her mouth.

"I forgot what I think stays in my head, if I say anything aloud it'll be heard through telekinesis."

Paul two turned around towards the gate Gwen stood and asked,

"Is anyone there?" as Paul two began to walk towards the gate.

"Shoot I gotta leave," she rushed as she forced her eyes open by stabbing herself with a knife she pulled out of her boot.

She looked around to see Paul had begun to charge the man as he screamed. The man pulled out a grenade while Paul pulled his sword from its scabbard.

"So that's his twin, a way more powerful Paul," she began thinking. "A man that could conquer anything, and if trained properly he could basically take anyone down. If the will of the cosmos is, however, that Paul is supposed to eventually fuse with his inner twin making them one, he could be unstoppable. A powerup to the point where your power is felt throughout the entire omni-verse, but a limit. Hm, there would also be consequences to this but when isn't there a consequence?" She asked herself.

Gwen looked up to see the man and Paul flying back and forth as their fists were hardly seen through the punching.

"Wait, if the will of the cosmos is for Paul and his team to become the most powerful, then why did my dad send minions after him. Also, why should I stay out of the fights?"

His heart was racing as he rapidly punched and dodged punches, trying to stop the amount of damage he was taking. His ribs bled internally as his arms began to ache from the multiple collisions of fist on fist.

Paul began to get distance, leaping backwards towards the goal post. This was a bad idea as the man pulled out a belt of grenades and a huge red ball.

"What is that?" Paul regretfully asked.

"A ball of C4, TNT, and basically anything that goes boom," he threatened in a deep voice. "I call it a bomb ball," he chippered as he threw the bomb ball and the belt of grenades at Paul.

"By the way," he chuckled as he turned around to walk away. "I pulled the pins three seconds prior to throwing it."

Staring at the ball of death, he put his right arm in front of his face as it blew up. The blast sent him flying over the school building and across streets before landing onto a yellow Winky Wacky Burgers.

Gwen began to chase the flying Paul as she ran out of the alley. She jumped on top of cars to get a better view but she lost him due to his landing.

"Shoot," she thought. "From the angle and trajectory, he should be," she pondered as she jumped off of the cars and began to run down the street into the direction he went.

"Obviously there," she mocked herself as she rounded the end of the street corner to see a building that seemed to have collapsed. "That should be him," she thought. "This must be the end of town, a neighborhood that borders the entire city. That's how I remember, but why is there a restaurant in front of these specific houses? Behind those houses should also be a few baseball fields, maybe we can lead the demon there."

She began to run towards the restaurant at full speed, pushing crowds of people away as they began to litter the parking lot in front of the restaurant.

"Shit that hurt," he thought as he rubbed his head. He stood up and glared at the hole he created. "This is so cool, a ball of explosives, a sword made specifically for me. I even got tossed like a real protector."

Pauls eyes glistened until a man grabbed his shirt, taking his attention away from the hole. As the man began to yammer on, he realized the man's breath smelled like a cigarette and his clothes were greasy. He looked behind him to see Sean and his eyes grew even bigger.

Then, he saw Gwen walk in pissed off. He could feel the hatred seeping from her dark purple aura.

"Hey, I don't know who you are," she warned as put a hand on the man's shoulder and stared him in the eyes. "But take your hands off of him. I don't want it to be uglier than it already is."

She began step away as the man began to tear his face apart from seeing demons being tortured in her eyes.

She walked over to Paul and jumped out onto the street outside as police sirens blared in the distance. The demon in the trenchcoat was waiting in front of a house behind the building.

"We gotta get them to a baseball field," Gwen rushed as she dragged him down the street towards the demon.

The demon began to walk towards a car parked in the house's driveway, causing the two to freeze in their steps. It picked the car and threw it towards the two, causing them to duck and zip past the demon.

Explosions were heard down the street as they ran towards a baseball field through an alley on the right.

"Why did you kill that man?" Paul annoyed as he gathered his footing and began to keep up with Gwen.

"Well, he did grab you by the shirt and we have no time for that. I'd rather have one die than an entire neighborhood," she belittled as they jumped a fence to a baseball field.

They looked back to see that the man disappeared, Paul looked above to see a long legged and armed red demon with horns slashing at him with his long and sharp demon axe. He pulled out his sword and blocked the attack quickly, causing the demon to stop mid air. They stood there in a standstill with their weapons crossed, until Paul pushed the demon away. The three stood there in a triangle while Gwen stood pressed behind Paul.

"I'll make sure to end you and this universe," began the demonic creature.

"You're here to be sent back," the man replied, pointing his sword. "I'm not here for discussion."

"Get him Bison," she professed as she shoved him a bit.

He felt himself fall asleep and regain consciousness with a new mindset, a battle strict mindset. He charged towards the demon with the swing of his sword and a strike towards his enemy. The demon responded by blocking it, causing Paul's sword to bounce backwards.

"Satin says hello," the demon taunted as they stood three feet between each other.

"Tell him I said, return to sender," Bison responded as he leaped towards the demon, slashing at his chest. He landed then jumped backwards to his original position.

"Cheap shot," growled the demon as he dragged his hand across his chest, staining his fingers with his own blood. He looked at his bloody fingers and began to get visibly angry.

"Maybe, but you're the one throwing grenades and cars," Bison replied as he caught his breath.

They began to charge each other and as the gap closed, their weapons clashed furiously as the air around them began to swirl. Rocks and dirt began to fly outwards like a spitting tornado, and the Earth beneath their feet began to crack and tear into a crater-like hole.

They threw each other around as they blocked and parried each other's attacks until Paul charged the demon with a sword jab. In response, the demon slammed his axe onto the ground, barely missing Paul as it left a scar straight down his chest. He backed away a bit to get distance before charging again with his sword held tightly in his right hand. In response, the demon slammed down his axe again, causing the ground and dirt to fly into the air as it split the ground.

Using the momentum, like the rocks thrown, Paul threw himself upwards with his swords handle held tight in his hand as he spun himself. The spin was shortened due to the swords blade crashing into the demon's skull. It collapsed to the ground as its head spouted black ooze.

"In order to actually kill it," Gwen began to talk to Paul telepathically. "You gotta cut its head off," she finished.

He stood over its body with his sword held high as he thought, "Isn't there another way?" he questioned as he pressed the sword against its neck, slicing it in half.

"The cops will be here any moment," Gwen assured as Paul looked around. "What's wrong?" she asked.

"The light revealed someone lying in the grass, they were watching," he began to walk towards the entrance of the baseball field before looking behind himself to see a cop sliding around the corner.

They climbed the fence and ran into an alley two blocks away and climbed up the right side of the fire escape. Gwen lifted the window and climbed inside to hide in her apartment twelve floors above the ground.

"I thought you lived on the other side of the street," he mentioned while they climbed.

"Well the four of us were born with a natural gift. Mine is having a hideout I can call anywhere. I don't even need to do anything, all I need to do is just think about it," she responded as she began to open the window and climbed in.

"So can you elaborate what this means?" He annoyingly asked as he climbed through the window himself.

"First," he turned around after shutting the window to see Gwen holding a bar of soap and a towel. "A shower, you smell like something hideous."

He gave her a blank stare, then they began to laugh as Paul accepted the offering.

"The bathroom is right outside of the door. If you need it bigger let me know," she chippered as she smiled.

"Right," he nervously as he walked out of the door into a four walled room with a door on the left. He turned the glass knob and opened the door to a very tiny bathroom. The toilet was so small that it was barely visible, and the sinks and shower were just as big.

"Wait," he thought.

"Yeah, I kind of forgot about the bathroom," she sighed as her head appeared from the open door.

The bathroom began to expand as the toilet, sinks, and the shower grew to normal size. The floor tiles and toilet were crisp and clean white. Along with the shower, that was big enough for two people, sat across from the dual sink with a large mirror behind it.

"Wow, she really likes the couple style," he began to think as he entered the bathroom and closed the door.

"Pretty neat huh?" She intervened into his mind.

"Can I get some privacy?" He squeaked in shock, dropping everything in his hands.

Gwen walked towards the dresser and opened a drawer in the top right and picked up a solid black book. She sat down in the chair and opened the book to a blank lined page and began writing in it.

"I've been observing Paul," it began. "He knows how to fight hand to hand, but a little training would never hurt. His natural talent hasn't shown itself yet, but I'm pretty sure it will if the events coming up should draw it out. Something else is odd, there is no information on his parents or where he came from. If I can find this out I can finally do a full observation of Paul. He also has a twin inside of his mind, it's like a switch when he needs to survive or protect," the door to the room opened, interrupting her writing.

"Hey," Paul intruded as he walked into the room. There was a towel on his waist, exposing his ripped upper body.

"You didn't take a long shower?" She asked, a bit disturbed.

"I mean, I get all of the important parts, you know. The arms, the legs, the feet, my face. Sometimes inside of my ear, but the water makes it feel weird."

"Whatever you say captain questionable. So, about your natural talent," she began as she closed her book, putting it back into the drawer.

"Right," Paul clarified as he began to put on his pants. "What is that exactly?"

She watched as he slipped each ripped leg into each pant leg.

"It's an ability that we take to each omni-verse, it doesn't drop like the natural abilities of the world's we leave and go to. As for me, no matter where we go, I could look at a building and want my hideout there. Like magic and a big poof, it'll appear. In total there are infinite ones to give to appointed protectors. The most mind-screwing part is that there will only be four protectors, and when they are killed, four more will be appointed."

"How do you know all of this?" He asked as he began to put on his shirt.

"Well, if I weren't here to give you information and be a protector's guardian, then who would push you to do what you're being called to do."

"You're from the underworld, so doesn't that make you a devil. Aren't devil's supposed to not have others do their bidding? So does that mean..."

"I'm not forcing you to do anything," she began. "I'm pushing you to do what's better for humanity and all beings. If I weren't here, you'd never have an excuse to care."

"Who can say I saved you because I cared? What if I did it because you needed to get out of that situation?" He argued.

"Then tell me why you took me away from my fathers clutches when you knew that I lived there my entire life. Even after that fact, you took an ass whooping just to prove you wouldn't back down. You stood in front of Satan himself, who could've killed you with a glare. You're just a mere mortal playing against immortals to prove a point that you don't fucking care? That's bullshit!" she exclaimed as excitement built inside of her.

As he put his right arm through his shirt, a faint whistle could be heard in the distance, getting louder and louder.

"What is that?" Paul began to ask as a rocket burst through the window, causing glass to spray everywhere as it flew into the side of his head. It exploded, sending Paul through the door on the right of him.

Gwen stood up immediately, knocking down her chair to run towards Paul who was lying unconscious and bleeding from the head.

"Shit," she panicked as she looked towards the window as adrenaline began to kick in.

Reaching her arm out and spreading her fingers apart, steps appeared out of the wall in front of them. She picked Paul up and placed him next to her side as she began to jog down the stairs. Rockets could be felt and heard hitting the house, like an ambush.

Gwen reached the bottom floor as explosions shook the building and sprinted out of the building. She ran into the open street, hoping to get away from the assault. To her surprise, the rockets stopped firing and there were no signs of enemies as she looked around.

"Cheap shot," she criticized as she gritted her teeth.

She walked to the TV store across the street and placed Paul against the wall. She reached for her pink bookbag realizing she left it inside, along with all of their gear.

"Good thing I have this," she reassured herself as she pulled a small red and white case out her boot. She pressed the button on top and threw it not too far away from herself. White smoke dispersed from the container like a small geyser as it spilled onto the ground. When the smoke cleared, her dresser was sitting on the sidewalk.

She walked up to the dresser and opened the bottom drawer, revealing her pink bookbag. She picked it up and walked over to the bloody Paul.

"The hideout should be restored by the end of the week," she reminded herself as she patched up Paul's face, wrapping a bandage around it. He began to regain consciousness.

"What happened?" He asked as he rubbed his head.

"You got hit by a rocket, your face was mostly uninjured. Other than a few cuts and scratches, you're surprisingly tough. What do you think it could've been?" She questioned as she sat next to him.

"I don't know," he began. "I didn't think I could survive something so powerful. You'd think that would blow half of my face off," Paul chuckled nervously.

Gwen began to think as she stood up to look into the TV store window with the news on it.

"Could it be his natural talent?" She thought as she began to pay attention to the news.

"Breaking news, there is currently a car chase in lower Skylark County where a male, Sean Baskins, is evading cops as he is speeding down the highway. It is unknown where he is off to in such a hurry, but he better stop before the cops get annoyed. That is all," the TV announced before cutting to static.

"Shit," Gwen thought. "If he's like his brother, he's going to make a dumb mistake."

She approached Paul and grabbed him by the arm, lifting him to his feet.

"We gotta go," Gwen pushed for time as she walked to her dresser and began rummaging through the items.

"What's going on?" Paul asked as she shoved his red mask to his chest.

"Your brother is probably going through some traumatic events right now, it's probably why he's being chased by cops," she rushed as she dressed herself in her vigilante costume.

Paul strapped his baldric to his waist and his sword in its scabbard as Gwen walled over to her dresser. She reached her hand behind the leg and pressed a button, causing the mirror to shrink down to a box.

"So where are we going?" Paul asked.

"To the police precinct. We're going to have to become enemies of the state if we want to live through this with everyone alive," she replied as she put the box in her boot and her book bag onto her back.

"Wait, do we even have a plan?" He asked as Gwen began to jog into the alley immediately to the right.

"We go in and ask nicely. If they don't give him to us," she answered as she began to sprint. "Then we'll have to take him by force, but we've gotta get there before Sean makes another dumb move."

Paul began to sprint, barely keeping up with her rapid legs as they ran throughout the night.

"How do you know all of this?" Paul questioned.

"I did my research," she responded as she entered an apartment complex.

"What're we doing, I thought we had to go to the police precinct," Paul assumed as he stood outside, rethinking everything.

Gwen stopped running up the stairs immediately in front of the door and began to talk with her back turned.

"Listen, I understand that just yesterday you were a regular human kid and now today you're a murdering psychopath. The truth is that you're not psychopathic, you've been abused and now your soul has had enough abuse from this world. You may not know it now," she assured as she turned around to walk down the stairs towards Paul.

"You cannot let the fear get to your head, regretting decisions is a daily basis occurrence in the underworld. Everyone there has already lived on this Earth or the Earths of another universe, not us. I'm just saying that those people are the ones who should be regretting their choices, not the men and women in the above world."

"But you can't tell me I'm not supposed to regret," Paul stifled as they stood at the bottom of the steps with the door open. The bright moon from the night poured into the abandoned building as they stood still with emotions running high.

"I never said that, I'm saying that you can't run around thinking of every little thing, it'll make you crazy. We don't have time for this," she finished as she turned around. "Either you're with me, the good guys, or with the bad guys when they catch you." She then began to sprint up the stairs towards the roof.

"That's unfair," Paul whispered as he began to run after her. "You never told me what we were doing," he shouted as he slowly trailed behind, huffing and puffing along.

"We're running on the rooftops," she shouted back as she shoulder bashed through a door, revealing a wide open rooftop.

Gwen looked to her left and then to her right before pointing to her left to say, "We're going this way, if we do this right we should be able to reach it in no time.

"Wait," Paul reached out and grabbed her arm, stopping her before she took another step. "We should have a plan, like maybe a backup plan to go with it. You know," he cringed as he took his hand away and rubbed his head. "So we don't go in and get shot dead."

Gwen turned around and approached Paul, grabbing him by both of his shoulders and staring through the eye holes in his mask.

"You're right," she agreed as she shook him out of excitement. "Come up with a plan, this will be your mental training," she exclaimed; letting him go as she sat on the ground.

"Well, what's the objective," he pondered as he sat next to her.

"To retrieve Sean and escape successfully."

"Right, so if we enter through the roof, we should be able to get in and out with a breeze. If we break the lock on the rooftop door, it'll be our entrance and exit," he explained as he stared at his shoes.

"So, what's the plan after that?" Gwen questioned.

"Alright, first; we cannot let anyone notice us. I'll lead the way, but we don't know where to find him, hmmm. Then that just means this intrusion is going to have to be a single man thing."

They sat in silence for a moment as Paul thought with the palm of his thumb pressed against his chin and Gwen swiped the air in front of her, looking at Paul as she asked.

"Should I get firearms?" she stared as a black and dark purple mix created a portal.

"No, but can people enter through there?" He asked, pointing at the portal.

"I think so, I've never truly tried it. The last time I did it, I was teleported into an armory where I got the guns. Though I was almost filled with bullets, I survived."

"Right," he hesitated. "We don't need them,, I'll go in and search for Sean while you stay atop the rooftop. If things go awry and Sean has already lost his mind, he will try to commit suicide by either jumping from the rooftop or a classic gunfight. The two questions humans keep in the back of their mind is to go out and die as a coward and jump to your death? Or do you die rebelling against those who brought you harm?" He asked himself as he stood up and prepared himself. "Are you ready?"

Gwen looked up with glee in her eyes as she put away her portal and stood up.

"Yeah, if we can do this fast enough, then we can get some sleep," she hoped.

They began to run across the rooftops, jumping over small gaps that overlooked small alleys below. Birds flew beside their masks as they sprinted towards the precinct with the moon shining brightly above. About two rooftops away, they noticed a group of people with guns, about twenty in front of a singular human.

"Here," Gwen ushered as she opened her portal mid run and pulled out a metal circle with a handle.

She tossed one to Paul as she looked over and instructed, "Deflect the bullets and we'll go with plan B."

He caught the shield and they began to rush towards the group of men, seeing the front line get shot dead while the second line of men readied themselves to the front. Bullets flew as the two jumped in front of the death embracing Sean and began to reflect bullets.

"Go," Paul commanded Gwen as they turned around and grabbed Sean. They began to jump across rooftops and duck under bullets.

"What're you guys doing?" Sean asked as they ran.

"We're saving you moron," Paul replied through his muffled mask as he hurtled over generators.

Gwen led the way as the two behind began to make a full sprint. They jumped over twenty rooftops before a helicopter stopped them in their tracks. The sound of caterpillar treads and thousands of feet filled the air as they approached a gap too wide to jump.

"Did they call in the army?" Paul asked as he looked down from the edge of the rooftop. Thousands of militia and militia vehicles were seen to litter the street for ten miles.

"What did you do?" Gwen asked as she walked over to Sean.

"I got a phone call from my girlfriend and somebody murdered her." Sean began. "I was trying to get to her before she was murdered, but I was too late. The cops caught up after I got there and beat the hell out of me, then they tried to pin the murder on me. So in response, I got angry and killed before commiting suicide."

"It wasn't suicide if you're still alive," Gwen badgered as she dragged the back of her hand across his face. "We saved you and all you can say is," she began as she grabbed him by the shirt.

The helicopters and militia stood by as they watched the feud from above, and through their visual transmitters being sent to the ground. Strict punishment was allowed unless there was a possibility that one criminal were to kill the other, going rogue. She dragged him to the end of the rooftop and held him above the tanks below.

"That you *committed* suicide. We saved your sorry ass and all you can do is waste away and complain…"

"Gwen, put him down," Paul reasoned as he walked towards her cautiously.

"You get in the way and you'll join him," she snapped, turning her attention back to Sean. His hands gripped her wrists with all his strength, she was surprisingly strong.

"Listen," Sean pleaded. "I was just saying that I just lost my girlfriend and child."

"Do you think I give a damn about your pity? There's millions of people going through difficult situations. These buildings that are about to collapse, they're apartment buildings. When the tanks shoot, every single civilian will be dead. The casualties will be in the near grand. Personally, I lost my home twice in less than twenty four hours.

"How does that happen you may ask? Well it's none of your business, but if I wanted you dead, or worse, I could because you and everyone in this world are weaker than me. I could gloat all I want, but I won't because gloating gets you killed. If you wanna die and suffer, tell me now," she finished as she let him go.

Paul lunged forward, throwing his body onto the ground with his hand outreached. He stretched over the ledge and grabbed Sean by the shirt in the nick of time.

Gwen walked away as she looked at the helicopter hovering above them. The man inside held a button to access a microphone that could be heard from up to six miles away.

"Make a move, and we'll drop you like a sack of potaters'," the man warned as it cut off.

She looked at the gap between the roof they stood on and the one next to them.

"This is a large gap, what do you say we do Bison?" Gwen asked.

"I say you jump over, we'll initiate plan B on my go. Even if I'm stranded," he reassured as he took another look down.

He sat with Sean against the edge to see four tanks at the base of the two possible buildings they could safely jump to.

"Alright, but how is that pussy getting across?" She asked, pointing at Sean.

"I'll throw him," he responded.

Sean began to freak out and complain as Paul walked up to him and grabbed him by the flailing arm. Gwen prepared herself by starting at the beginning of the roof, sprinting to the end and jumping, barely catching the ledge. She pulled herself up and gave Paul the thumbs up. He looked at Sean as they stood up and prepared him,

"Are you ready?"

He spun the complaining Sean around like a spinning top before letting his body rapidly spin through the air. Gwen caught the spinning man and looked over at Paul, who was still on the opposing rooftop. He prepared himself to run when suddenly, a dozen deafening shots rang out into the air, sending the buildings tumbling down. The building Gwen stood on began to collapse into the building which Paul was standing on.

"Plan B, just go without me," he yelled as Gwen opened a portal with Sean under her arm and jumped in.

Paul finished his run as the ground crumbled beneath him, launching him towards the side of the building Gwen had left. He began to slide down smoothly as he looked up to see a helicopter shooting at the windows below. He smashed a cracked window with his feet, making him free fall inside. He pulled out the grappling hook from his sword's handle and shot it out of the window above him, hooking onto an object Paul was unaware of. When the building fell, Paul was to be seen hanging from a helicopter as it spun out of control from the extra weight.

It caused the helicopter to nearly miss a building, crashing Paul right into the side. He coughed up blood and proceeded to push onwards, swinging on the rope with all of the strength left inside of him. He vaulted upwards into the helicopter, sending three men to their deaths. He tried to regain control, but it was too late and he had to make a skydive out of the helicopter to attempt to survive. Suddenly, a portal appeared and swallowed him whole.

Chapter 9

The offer

He landed onto his side with a thump, looking up, he couldn't see anything but the smell of rotten food. He patted the ground around him to feel for walls and began to think this was Gwens' doing, but when he called out, there was no answer.

"Where am I?" he thought as he sat there for what seemed like five minutes.

A light flicked onwards in front of Paul, who was leaning onto his hands, revealing a humongous seven foot giant in a red swivel chair. His hair was a proper blonde and slicked back to his ears as his smile gave Paul chills. A desk was seen in front of the giant with rotten apples and papers scattered about the wood.

Paul trembled to his feet as his body still ached from the police chase. Paul stared at the man with little to no energy in his bones. His mask was cracked slightly and his arms ached with pain, he was in no shape to fight. The man arose from his seat, growing a few more inches as he began to tower Paul. He held a humongous white cat in his cradled arms.

"Such a cliché," he thought as the man approached him, every footstep shook the ground and Paul to the bone.

Standing face to chest, the man bent down to meet Paul's gaze.

"So," Scorch placidly said as he stared into Pauls' frightened face. "You're the new hero around here?" His voice was deep and treacherous.

"I don't even know what's going on," Paul thought as he smelled the man's surprisingly minty breath.

"I'll give you a deal," the man proposed as he stood up and walked over to his desk. He put down the kitten and gave it a nice long rub against its spine. "Leave the human-devil child, and join me. The cops would be no problem and as you can currently see, I have similar powers to Gwen. Being from the underworld myself, I know more than her," he walked behind his desk over to his chair and picked it up as he continued talking.

"I was once helping a human who had great intentions for the world, but in the end, she betrayed me," he pitied as he put the chair in front of Paul and sat down with his legs crossed. "It's been several years but I became a principal soon after the incident to forget the pain I endured. I thought that maybe I could give someone a smile that I lost when I was a good samaritan," he blabbering as Paul began to get frustrated with all of the lies and began to interrupt.

"Listen," Paul contested as he gained courage. The man gave a look of recognition as he let Paul talk.

"These sentences that you're making up are starting to piss me off. Either tell me the truth or else," Paul warned as he gripped his fists.

"Are you going to fight me?" The man began to give an echoing laugh as put his hands on his knees. "Fine, since I don't feel like tossing you around, I'll tell you the truth. If you try to stand against me, you will die like the rest of them. If you join me, however, I will make you into a great servant of mine. You could rule the cosmos with all of that hidden potential inside of you, and I could be your king," he bargained as he stood up and walked circles around Paul with his hands folded behind his back.

Paul began to think of all the possibilities before he began to laugh hysterically, laughing and laughing before giving a small, light cough. The man grabbed Paul and chucked him against the wall, almost squishing him on impact. He tried to recover, but the man appeared in front of him like instant teleportation, grabbing him like a doll and tossing him to the other side of the room. He hit the wall with a loud thud as cement pieces flew off from behind his body.

"You know, I never had a true reason to defend the cosmos against cowards like you," he coughed as he slid down the wall and blood poured from his mouth.

"Hearing that made me realize something hilarious," Paul criticized as he began to cut his palm with his nails. "I'm not one for sob stories, or stories at all, but if only you knew what I had to go through in my home life. The weight of guilt I felt every time I lied for a monster that didn't care about me nor my brother.

"Because of this fact, I realized that the fear I feel now doesn't even compare to the five year old me hearing my brother get abused. Wondering if maybe, just maybe, if I did whatever she wanted I wouldn't get that treatment. And then the weight of knowing I'm betraying the only man that held the key to my family. I've gotten so used to the fear and corruption in my head, I'm numb to it. I feel like I can fight anything," he lectured as he stood up and the air around his feet began to spiral.

The tall man began to give a questionable expression as he backed away.

"What is that?" the man thought as Paul rambled away at the fact he loved animals. He charged Paul, attempting to stop him from getting any more hyper.

Paul sidestepped the punch Scorch threw in the middle of his teleport. Bison then punched him with his left fist, indenting his knuckles into his skull. Scorch responded immediately with a right until they began to fight at the speed that was too fast for human eyes to see.

"This wasn't supposed to happen," Scorch chippered as he threw a heavy right hook. Paul grabbed his arm and tilted it upwards as they began to converse.

"I think I get it," Paul began as they stood there.

Scorch tried prying his arm from the grip as Paul rambled.

"I used to love playing silent video games. You know, the ones where you have to be stealthy in order to secure the kill?" He let go, causing the man to tumble backwards and fall.

"If I wanna connect with my twin, I'm going to have to switch my mindset from Paul to Bison. I get it now," he realized as he looked at his hands, crunching them open and closed.

"Wh….wh…who are you?" the man stammered as Paul closed his eyes.

The air in the room became too dense for normal lungs to breathe as the air around Paul began to set fire. It fluctuated between wind and fire before the wind dispersed the fire, leaving a spiral of wind around Paul.

"I think the woman that is in love with me gave me the name Bison, yeah, Bison. I like that name," he remembered as the ground began to crack with every step he took towards the feared Principle.

Gwen clutched her head in agony as her and Sean were walking towards a shelter on the other side of town. She buckled to her knees, screaming in pain as she clutched her head.

"What's going on?" Sean asked, stopping beside her.

"Paul, he's powered up. I can't explain it, but his natural talent and the connection between him and I affects me somehow." She stopped clutching her head and began to stare off in front of her as she realized the impossible.

Whilst they stood just a few feet apart from each other, Bison began to walk towards the scared Principle, who was backing up to the wall that was stained with Paul's blood. The aura he felt plunged him into immense deep fear, one he's never felt before.

"I know your truth, the fact that you want to destroy this omni-verse for a reason I do not know nor will understand. If you want my honesty, I would rather sit by and sip on tea like an Englishman. Then again, I don't want my house blown to bits."

"They call him Bison?" A tall woman wearing a yellow flower dress and white high heels asked as she stood next to a man in a red robe over omni-verse fourteen. "Who is he exactly?"

"From my records, he's a very powerful kid, and so are the other three. Omni-verse fourteen has a lot of potential, it would be a great shame to erase this one as well. There's also a woman named Gwen who arose from the underworld to be closer to this Bison man," he observed as a screen stood in front of him, displaying Bison's current actions as he fought the Principle.

"So, the preparations are complete?" She urged.

"There's still one man who doesn't know, his human name is Byron. I really like that name," he chuckled as he smiled. "If these men are prepared, make them into warriors, then I will train them myself."

She nodded, turning into a yellow ball as she shot herself downwards into the omni-verse, disappearing with a flash.

Bison huffed and puffed as his chest inflated and deflated rapidly. They stood in front of each other while Bison held his sword tired-like. The Principle had no scars.

"*What* are you?" Bison pondered as he casually spat blood from behind his mask.

"I could ask you the same," Scorch gasped with a short breath. "I've been pummeling you for at least twenty minutes, how are you standing?" He asked as he clutched his left arm in pain.

"This body is able to do so much more," Bison short-breathed as he fell to a knee, stabbing his sword into the ground.

"So, are you Paul or the spirit of someone else?" The Principle wondered.

"In all reality, I am a soul created by Pauls' fuel for battle. It was so intense it kind of split off from his soul and made me, or so I believe." he replied with a smirk.

"So, you're telling me that Paul made a version of himself out of his own soul?"

"It's a possibility," Bison taunted as he stood to his feet. "So are you ready to finish this battle? I think I'm finally getting the hang of this," he stated as he stretched his shoulder.

"No," The Principal screamed as he hastily ran to the elevator that was directly behind him. "You can adapt in battle, even after you've been beaten to a pulp. I'm out of here," he fretted as he pressed the button rapidly..

The dual doors opened to allow Scorch to escape, but when he turned around, he saw Bison standing in the elevator. The eye holes behind his mask glowed crimson as shoved Scorch out of the elevator and followed him.

"Done playing already?" Bison asked as he teleported in front of the helpless man.

Bison walked within arms reach of the man, preparing himself to pick him up when Scorch suddenly charged him. He pushed Bison backwards into the elevator, causing it to shake as the doors closed. He sat against the wall with a few broken ribs as he watched the Principle search his clothes.

"You fell into my trap," Scorch mocked as he desperately pulled out a syringe.

"There's no possible way you could've known," Bison uttered as the man stabbed himself with the needle.

Bison began to rapidly look around the enclosed elevator room, only to find one button for the ground floor. Scorch began to convulse on his feet, screaming and kicking violently as he shook himself to the ground. His body began to glow green and expanded as his skinny muscle arms were bloating.

"What the hell," Bison pondered as the elevator shook rapidly, rattling like a baby's toy.

It seemed as if forever had passed until they'd reached the ground floor. As Scorch stood onto his feet, composing himself, he was three times bigger and was no longer a skinny athletic guy. This man was a brute.

Bison had nowhere to run with his back against the wall as the man reached his big, meaty hand towards Bison. He stabbed it with his sword and Scorch ignored it, absorbing the blade into his skin.

"What the he-" Bison panicked as the man grabbed him by the torso, flinging him backwards through the double elevator doors.

The dual metal doors bursted wide open, causing Bison to crash onto the floor and slide like a hockey puck that's just been smacked. His body stopped on what felt like a spiky curb.

Looking up, Bison could see about fifteen demons looking down onto him as their eyes were filled with murderous intent. Putting himself into a ball position, Bison tried to protect himself to the best of his ability as they stabbed him with daggers and kicked him harshly. Scorch began to walk towards the group as his feet smashed the ground with every barefoot step.

"Did you really think," he bellowed with a deep, disturbing voice. "That you could stand up to me?" He asked as he began to laugh nonchalantly, preying onto the beaten Bison.

Frustrated, Bison began to think of the escape routes available to him, or what was at his disposal.

"There's about twelve, no, thirteen maybe," Bison began to think as he hurled into a ball. Blood began to leak from his already frail body as he focused.

"I can feel something, like a bunch of energy being collected into one specific area," he thought as his body began to vibrate. "It's too much to handle, I've gotta let it out," he unrolled and jump-crouched to his feet.

He threw his arms outwards as he roared so deep it shook the ground, stopping the brute in his tracks. An energy shockwave dispersed outwards, colliding with all of the demon's preying onto Bison. A few were cut in half while the others were missing limbs.

"I'm tired of your games!" Bison exclaimed as his eyes glowed black. "I will kill you," he grumbled as the air beneath his body began to spiral, lifting his feet from the ground.

The floor cracked from immense pressure as the walls began to cave inwards. Wind erupted from Bison like some sort of tornado was being formed.

The air whipped violently, lifting Scorch from his feet as fear overtook his body. He couldn't understand how someone so weak could be strong, it was unimaginable.

Suddenly, a bright light blinded them both, making them cover their eyes as they fell to the floor with a thud. The air in the room stood still as the brute was stuck where he laid with his back onto the ground.

A woman in a yellow dress stood in between the brute and Bison, who was seeping anger from his bloody and bruised body.

"This is not a fight for now," she began to say with a soft voice. "If you guys take yourselves any further, the entire city will be enveloped into a storm." She warned as she waved her flowery staff in front of the brute, sending out pink smoke as they disappeared.

Chapter 10

The awakening

The night was still young as Gwen and Sean walked down the street hoping to run into Paul.

"Maybe he was caught," Sean predicted, breaking the silence.

"Maybe. That just means we're going back to the police station," Gwen replied as she angrily walked within the night.

"Wait, I just got out of there. I don't want to go back," he worried.

"Who cares, if it comes to it I'll leave you there. Don't forget who saved your sorry ass," she pestered as she began to walk faster.

Attempting to keep up, Sean began to jog as he talked. "Okay, maybe I was a little rash,"

"What're you even good at?" She asked, interrupting him. "If you're going to be on the team, then you gotta be useful."

"Wait, so you're a part of that thing I saw at the restaurant?" he questioned as he kept pace.

"I don't know what you're talking about," she replied, annoyed.

"I have to know I'm not going to die or something. What was he talking about? Me being the one to defeat the Low Priest?"

"What?" She stopped walking and turned towards Sean. "You got a message? Then that means I was right. It was just an educational guess on who it was and now that I definitely know it's you, I feel bad for us," she taunted as something behind Sean, in the distance, caught her attention

"Hm," she let out as she thought. "Maybe, just maybe, if we remove his 'bitch' side, we could get to the petrified warrior beneath."

Gwen stared at the full beautiful full red moon in the sky. She enjoyed the moon because of how much it affected the water and the seas. Suddenly, a bright yellow light shone in the sky, turning the nighttime into day for a short period of time.

It landed in front of the two, blinding them immediately as they raised their arm to block the light.

"I'm sorry," a lady that stood in front of them apologized in a sweet, concerning voice. She was accompanied by a man in a red mask.

Gwen dropped her arm, squinting to make out an image of a man in a cracked red mask standing next to a woman in a yellow dress.

"Bison?" Gwen blurted.

"Sorry I didn't just pick up your friend to drop him off. We need to have a serious conversation," she pestered as she began to walk away.

Sean uncovered his face, realizing that they were leaving him behind as the others followed the woman.

"Hey," he yelled, making everyone stop in their tracks.

"What's wrong?" The woman asked as they turned around to listen to Sean.

"What the hell is going on? I don't know these two masked fellows, and you just popped up like a blazing sun," he complained.

"Even your arguments are nice," Gwen taunted.

"Let him talk," the woman interrupted.

"I enjoyed my life at the Winky Wacky Burgers. Sure it was low pay and the grease burned my arm, but those people were my friends and you guys could have killed them. And you," he glared, giving Gwen a death stare. "You killed my manager, he was a good friend. Yet, now you guys are telling me I'm supposed to be a warrior? What kind of horseradish is that?" he nagged.

Gwen took a step forward before she converted into a discussion.

"So you are the guy from that restaurant," she began as she walked closer towards Sean. "If he didn't look into my eyes, he wouldn't have done that to himself. The only beings that can handle that much pressure are beings from the underworld and probably deities who killed for the fun of it. All I'm saying is, if a person gets in my way, I will eliminate them immediately," she snarled, now face to face with the scared Sean.

He stood there as his legs shook rapidly. Bison and the lady were standing ahead of them, carefully observing.

"So what? You want me to just forget all the bull that happened in the past eight hours. I had a life, a girlfriend that was soon to be my bride and the mother of my child. She's dead because of this shit. WHY! WHY!" he repeatedly screamed over and over until he buckled to his knees with his face in his hands. "I can't tell you how broken I was," he sobbed. "I fought in the army, I served my country, why is this happening to me?"

Paul walked past Gwen to Sean and knelt down to gently place his hand on his shoulder.

"Look at me," he commanded in a muffled voice.

Sean sniffled his tears away and put his hands down, staring the masked man in the face.

"If you want to know the truth?" He began as he put his hands behind his head. "I'm not just a random masked fellow," he assured as he untied the knot behind his head, letting his mask fall to the ground.

Seans eyes widened in shock and glee, but mostly anger.

"Paul? What the hell! How is it that I'm stuck with you?" He complained.

Paul reached down to pick up his mask, turning it over and placing it against his face as he tied it back on. Gwen began to walk closer towards Sean, pissed off.

"That's your brother," she lectured as Paul walked back to the lady's side, ashamed.

"He has all the right to hate me Gwen," Paul reasoned. "I betrayed him in dire situations, it did not matter whether or not I had no control. Hardly any memories of the past is a terrible foe to face."

"Don't give me that shit," she corrected. "Who cares what he did, that's your brother. Whether or not he had total control in that situation, that's your brother and because your brothers, you are the men that mold each other. You mold him like he molds you, and just like you two mold the other brother, he does the same. Without you, he has no guidance to his true self, and without your other brothers, you are without guidance.

"He was tough because he learned from you on what not to do and what to do. You taught him more than you can give yourself credit for and all you can do is spite your younger brother. What was going on in his mind when he saw you getting tortured. Fear? Anger? Despair? This shit gets hard, but no matter what, you have each other. It saddens me deeply to see families fight," she finished.

Sean began to stare into space, understanding everything she was saying.

"Go apologize to him, and Paul," she commanded, turning to look at Paul. "You apologize to Sean for all of those years you've put him through what felt like hell, we cannot move on until you do. If we do, then everything will fall in the midst of battle, then we're all dead."

Sean nodded and stood to his feet, he took twelve steps towards Paul and hugged him unexpectedly.

"I'm not one for this," he assured as Paul hugged him back awkwardly. "But you need to know that it felt like you were on the enemy team those nine years I lived there. I'm sorry."

"Look," Paul began as he pushed him away. "I'm not one for hugs, or anything closely romantic, but I do accept your apology. I apologize for being a total dick."

They both laughed as Sean wiped the tears away.

"I love and hate these moments," Gwen observed as she looked over to the lady who was smiling from ear to ear. "What's her deal?" she thought.

"We have to go," the lady hurried, returning to her serious face. "If we stay too long, we'll be swarmed by demons. They know I'm here," she informed as she looked around at the rooftops before picking one. "There, we'll get on that rooftop and talk."

They began to cross the street when a garbage truck was seen barreling around the corner they were closest to. It charged towards them as they stood less than mere feets away from the truck. Suddenly, time seemed to have slowed down rapidly, like it had stopped in place. A yellow ball was seen to shoot through the sky, landing onto a faraway rooftop.

They collapsed onto the roof as time suddenly started again, as if it never happened.

"Is everyone okay?" The woman in the yellow dress asked.

"What the hell?" Paul began.

"I stopped time and teleported us here, there were about forty demons compacted into the garbage trucks' hopper. Now the question remains, were those demons after Paul or me?" She curiously pondered.

"Well, why would there be demons after you?" Gwen asked.

"Sometimes when I enter into a universe, I'm detected immediately by Scorchs or the enemy's army. This entire world is brutal, but we need to get back on topic. Does anybody know where I could find your third brother?"

"Wait," Sean interrupted. "How and why can demons fit into a hopper like that?"

"They're immortal unless you split the spine on their neck. You can crush the windpipe and the spine all you want, but it's flexible to the extent where I think they can't break it."

"So that's why I had to cut its head off?" Paul asked as he removed his mask and sat down with his legs crossed.

"Yes, because if you cut any other part off, it'll just grow back. In the real world, demons are immortal mortals. They're completely immortal in the afterlife though," the lady in the yellow dress informed.

"What the hell is going on?" Sean asked as he clutched his head in confusion.

"So I wouldn't have won when I went to hell, would I?" Paul asked Gwen as she stood next him with her arms across her chest.

"No, because the demon you thought you killed, was actually still breathing. In fact, if you look back you'll see he got up and joined the fray." Gwen bantered.

"That's messed up," he agreed through a laugh.

"Truly is," she responded as she sat down with her legs crossed. She began to untie her mask when Paul put a hand on her arm.

"Are you sure?" He asked, stopping her.

"Yeah," she proceeded as she looked over. "I can put a layer over my eyeballs if you don't want anyone to kill themselves," she suggested.

"Sure," he encouraged.

Her eyes began to turn pure black, covering her pupils.

"Creepy," the woman in yellow cringed. "Anyway, we have to get back on topic," she refocused as she stood in front of everyone. "Do you all know why we're here?" She asked, teacher-like.

"Well, doesn't it have something to do with protecting the omniverse?" Gwen asked.

"Sort of," she agreed, snapping her fingers. She made a black board appear behind her and a single piece of chalk in her hand. She began writing furiously, causing the chalk to break with every touch of the white board.

"You are here to protect not just this omniverse, but every omniverse in our existence," she lectured as she wrote. "If there is to be a suspicion of an enemy, we will send you into that universe to watch and observe until events occur. Even if things go awry, you shall stand by and not intervene with the main protagonist until they are too weak to fight. Then, you three, soon to be four, go and defend. The enemies that we are sending you to are not only universal level, those are for the heroes that can handle it. We are sending you to multiversal to omni-versial threat level enemies. If the situation gets too dire, then you will start fighting in the middle of the omni-iverse you stand in."

"What about a thing called natural talent?" Paul interrupted.

"Right, I thought it was already explained, that's okay. A natural talent, for those who don't know, is an ability within each of you that does not get dropped when you enter into another omni-verse. Let me explain," she interrupted Sean, who was about to speak.

"When you exit this omni-verse and enter into a different one, you'll enter a space and time rift. You'll either be sent back into time, or into the future, gaining the knowledge from the Earth we send you into to use on your own in battle. These battles could be life threatening, actually, all of them are. Therefore, we need to find all of your natural talents. You," she picked as she pointed her staff that she picked up from the whiteboard chalk holder at Gwen.

"You are a human demon that escaped from the underworld because of him," she lectured, pointing her staff at Paul. "Yours is ki, I saw it when you almost sent the city into a horrid storm."

Gwen perked up in excitement as she began to think. "That's so cool, that means his power could possibly be limitless."

"No, that doesn't mean his power is infinite Gwen. In a mortal coil, Paul can only gain the power of one to two multiverses if we train him. In his current state, he could call a universe to give him power when he gets annoyed or angry. In reality, his soul is capable of holding about an omni-verse worth of energy that could drive anyone mad. Sean," she brushed off, pointing her staff at Sean.

"I'm giving you a natural talent beside your own. You are a sharp shooter who doesn't miss a shot. Raised in a marine household, then actually being a marine, you have learned how to precisely hold a gun. That, however, is only good for sniping and a normal human could do it if they tried hard enough." Her staff began to glow red, sending a ball spiraling into Seans body.

"What the hell?" he asked as he patted his body all over.

"I give you another natural talent, being a pure brute. On Earth, it won't activate for another twenty four hours. In space, it activates immediately."

"What's Byrons?" Paul asked.

"I must not tell you, for he is something else of the matter. Anyway, onto the next topic. If you don't want to die, then you will listen to me. There are a few serums that Mr. Scorch invented, if one is injected into the ground, there could be a virus that can survive the harsh reality of space. If not dealt with properly, the omni-verse will be erased. We need a leader for this team, did I fail to mention?" She asked, turning away from the blackboard to face the group.

"Not me," Paul excluded himself.

"Nor I," Gwen also excluded herself.

"Well, someone has to do it," the lady pressured while Sean sat in silence.

"Wait," Paul began. "I should have asked you this sooner, but there was no time. Who are you really?" He asked in suspicion.

"I am the guidance of your team and if I go down, the entire omni-verse field could be at risk. Oh, that reminds me," she included, turning back to the chalkboard.

"Omni-verses have numbers, and there is only one that you guys should never enter when you need an Earth to crash at. Omniverse numbers help us determine which omni-verses have a universe threat or a multiverse threat. Omni-verse number one thousand ninety four. If you guys dare to step foot, Bison will be immediately detected and attacked because of his ki."

"Can you tell me how Paul split his soul?" Gwen asked.

"Well, the truth of the matter is, when Paul put his battle strict mind to the side, he split his personality. Now, you cannot mix up spirit splitting and mind splitting. Spirit splitting is when there are two living souls inside of one body. Mind splitting is when you split your personality into two mindsets, one that the person hates, and one that the person accepts. Now, in the case of Paul, his battle mindset was so strong that it turned into inner energy Paul himself could not access. That inner energy, we believe when fused with a fragment of a soul, has the possibility to create a second independent spirit, thus creating Bison, his closest enemy/ally."

"But how was it turned into inner energy, is it just the fact that his mindset was so strong it somehow created an energy made from his will to fight?" Gwen asked.

"Somewhat. It could be from a separate hidden energy already hidden within him, now Sean. I gave you the ability to withstand about a few multiverses of damage. In your current human state, being a protector is out of your wits. You really need to gain courage, like what you felt in that high speed police chase," the lady lectured.

"How do you know all of this?" Sean asked.

"Me and my husband watch over the omni-verses, we have the ability to display anything of interest with a screen. For example, when we sense an omni-verse stress level of energy on one Earth, we immediately identify said Earth and send protectors there to defend it. As per say, my husband and I were watching Bison fight Scorch, it was very interesting. Sean, you shot down twenty cops in one clip, your accuracy is incredible. How?" She pestered.

"Well, I was in the marines, as mentioned earlier. The sergeant wouldn't allow losers or anyone who couldn't land a shot. I knew I had to learn to shoot fast, so I went to the range and tried all of the rapid fire weapons first. Well, my sergeant was actually a decent guy at this moment when he told me, 'If you want to land every shot, learn with a single rate weapon first, then move onto the assault weapons.'

"So I adjusted. Using a pistol I learned to miss next to zero shots with the iron sight alone. I eventually began to use rapid fire guns, but the company made a specific gun I like to keep in my house. It's a single fire rate assault rifle, with every pull of the trigger the user could immediately fire another shot afterwards. So, I learned to be accurate with all types of weapons," he explained as everyone sat in shock.

"Impressive. Anyway, now that we had everyone explain themselves, or somewhat," the lady began.

"We need to move on because today I am going to meet up with both of you guys' brother Byron. I think I have an accurate location, all I need to do is put myself into the public eye as an idol, then have Byron defend me. I'll explain it all before him and I leave in a taxi or some getaway car. We will most definitely be assaulted again, so we're going to need you three on standby. When I collect Byron, we're going to need to hurry and regroup. There's no telling when Scorch is going to activate the serum, since somebody showed him he can be beaten. We'll meet on the highest rooftop, it's only accessible by stairs so this will be a test of endurance.

"Unfortunately I have to disable all of my abilities in this current state to become a mere human like one of you, so don't expect me to save you when you need it. I'll be as helpless as you guys without my abilities. After that, we will take a helicopter to Scorch's hideout where we take him down. Kill him at any cost, protect the citizens and try to not make collateral damage.

"Remember, we are only here to protect, not to show off. I'm talking to you, Bison," she glared looking into Paul's eyes. "If you don't control your twin, me and my husband will. He's not going to be nice nor care."

"Pssh," Paul spat. "I don't know what you're talking about."

"Listen," she evaluated. "You're suffering from something horrendous, a disorder where you not only have a split personality, but you also have a split soul. Having both sides fighting constantly can result in blind rage and irreparable damage. So, I'm going to appoint Gwen by your side no matter what, it's already been shown she is your main controller. Sean, you will be the one to shoot if things go awry, grab your gun."

The team stood up and began to walk to the edge or the roof before the lady stopped them.

"Wait," she pleaded with her hand stretched outwards in their direction. "Gwen, I forgot to give you this."

She put down her hand and lifted her staff, shooting her with a white ball.

"When Bison goes out of control, your second natural talent is to be a container. Basically, you can control the flow of energy particles with your aura and mind. It's hard to explain but if Bison ever starts destroying planets, you can send out your aura to stop the expansion of the energy blast. Neutralizing any effects that go along with it, it's very important to the mission."

"Wow, I don't know what to say," Gwen stammered, trying to be nice. "Why would you do this? Is it because you don't care I'm a demon, or is it because I'm protecting someone you love?'

"I believe you said to Paul the other hour, the name of your team, I like it. The Multiverse Warriors, yeah, it has a nice ring to it. Sean, what's your nickname?' she asked.

"Call me Bull, because they're always angry," he responded.

"It's because you know you're a brute, I like it." she winked. She then stabbed her staff into the ground, standing straight with a serious smile. "Multiverse Warriors, go out and protect this city and Earth at all costs. If things go awry, group up," she winked before she dismissed them with a light swing of her staff.

They jumped off of the rooftop, heading towards the radio tower on top of a one hundred floor building in the South.

Chapter 11

The war of humanity

They were a few streets away from the radio tower when Gwen pulled both Sean and Paul into an alley.

"You need a mask," she insisted as she knelt down to reach inside of her boot, pulling out her mysterious container.

"What is that?" Sean asked as she tossed it in his direction.

Catching the mysterious container, Sean fell backwards due to its weight. The container exploded as he was engulfed in smoke, revealing a dresser atop of Sean.

"Ow," he winced. "It doesn't hurt much, but you got a heavy ass dresser on my chest," he complained and struggled as Gwen bursted into laughter.

"Gwen, come on," Paul pleaded. "Are you hurt?" He asked as he walked to the dresser and lifted it with little effort.

"A little, but seriously, why?"

"Because I needed to laugh," she bantered as she walked over to her dresser.

She opened up the mask drawer and told him to pick between two masks, a blue and a black one. He reached for the blue mask that laid next to the black mask when Gwen grabbed his wrist, stopping his hand from extending further.

"You can't put your hand in there, humans will be literally erased. Your soul and body would become one with the universe," she warned as she let go, reaching into the dresser.

"Why?" Sean asked curiously.

"Well, have you ever heard of the fact that this is mine and only mine? Well, I took it to the extreme, anyone who attempts to remove any object from this dresser will be dealt with properly," she responded as she gently pulled out the blue mask. "One of my favorite colors," she pondered as she offered the mask to Sean.

"Well, what's your favorite color?" Sean asked as he accepted the mask.

"You don't need to know," she ignored as she walked back to her dresser and opened up the bottom drawer, revealing an assault weapon.

She picked up the assault rifle and tossed it to Sean.

"This will be for if we get invaded," she cautioned as she walked back to her dresser, pressing the button to reshape it.

"Are you guys ready? We have a lot of preparations, like climbing those steps before the other two arrive." Gwen walked over to Paul, standing next to him.

"Alright," Paul agreed as he turned towards the empty street. "Let's climb that tower and regroup to take down Scorch."

"Paul," Gwen whispered. "Before we move on, there is something I need to know."

"What is it?" He asked.

"Well, I went into your head the other hour and saw you as Paul, not Bison, being beaten by Bison. Why?" She boldly pestered.

He let out a sigh before dropping his head to stare at the ground.

"It's not something I can control anymore," he replied in a depressed tone. "All I know is that when Lucyfer had us trapped, I began to love war until I realized I might have to kill one day. Putting those emotions aside allowed my mind to go crazy with ideas, since nobody was dousing the flame. So in my theory, we fight because I hate to kill, while he'd rather see the world burn."

"So, he's an enemy?" She pressed.

"Not entirely, if we can come to an agreement he might help."

"That makes sense, are you okay?" She hesitated.

"Yeah, as for now. Sean," he brushed off as he looked back at Sean, who was fumbling with his mask.

"How do you put this thing on?" He struggled as he attempted to untangle the knot.

"Unknot it and tie it around the back of your head," Paul answered.

"Got it," Sean chirped, untangling the mask and putting it on properly.

"Let's go," Paul commanded as the three stepped out of the alley, turning right towards the courthouse.

As they walked, the night began to turn into day as the sun peaked its yellow bright bald head over the buildings.

"We've been awake all night?" Sean asked, walking behind Gwen and Paul.

"Apparently," Paul responded. "It has to be about five in the morning right now, has anyone been keeping time?"

"We don't keep time, time keeps us," Gwen bantered. "Also, I don't think we'll be sleeping too often when we're done with this."

"I like to sleep," Sean moped. "Wait, so in between missions, we can sleep right?"

"If we aren't getting ambushed by enemies who've noticed us entering their universe, or even worse, an extraterrestrial being that lives in the space of the onmi-verse," he assured Sean. "Also, Gwen and I agreed to make you the leader. You're smarter, you're going to be stronger, and you can coordinate when you're not being a pussy."

"Why me? I've only been in the marines, not the galactic patrol," Sean complained.

"That's also another reason why," Gwen intruded.

"Wait," Paul pondered, stopping at the base of the steps that lead to the extremely tall building. "This damn building's a courthouse too? That tells you a lot about this city," he mocked, placing a foot onto the step.

The door to the courthouse swung wide open, barely keeping the door on the hinges. A man in an orange police uniform was seen before being heard, holding an assault rifle in target mode.

"The courthouse is closed," the man warned with a crappy cop voice. "Why do you step here?"

Gwen began to talk as she stepped next to Paul, who interrupted before she could speak.

"We have important business with the cops, we need their help and we cannot find the police station. Could you maybe help?" Paul asked politely.

"Why are you masked? Uncover your faces," the officer commanded as he stepped closer.

"That is of no concern," Paul threatened as his eye turned white, scaring the man into lowering his weapon. "We need the help of police because there will be an invasion by terrorists," he convinced as he slightly grinned.

"What're you doing?" Sean began. "There might be a zombie invasion and you're telling him that it might be a terrorist? You shou-" he was shortly interrupted by a kick from Gwen, making him kneel to the ground while clutching his groin.

"How many," the cops asked as he holstered his weapon onto his back.

"We don't know, there could be thousands. We know that they'll be heading here any moment now to target this courthouse. They say the legal system is screwed, so they're screwing you," he explained.

"How do you know this?" The cop asked.

"Well, we are three humans in masks. We're basically vigilantes, except our job is to report it to the police. See, the thing is, this is the first time we've actually got intel like this. It's usually cats being stuck up trees and children in wells."

"Alright," the male officer listened as he reached for the radio on his shoulder. "Unit nine, army base," he spoke into the radio as it cackled in and out.

After a few short seconds, the radio began to static as a female voice was heard from the box.

"Army base nitro of the Skylark county, this better be a serious matter officer," she warned.

"There is a suspicion of multiple terrorists incoming from the far West of the Winky Wacky Burgers, the entrance of Skylark. They'll also be incoming to southeast of the Skylark Everything School, and East of the police district," he informed as he let go of the button.

"Are you speaking of the courthouse?" the radio asked.

"Affirmative," he confirmed with a stern expression.

"We'll have twelve units of land destroyers and five units of air to your location. Do you have an approximate time, or is this happening currently?" She questioned.

"We know it's going to happen before the opening of the courthouse. I have three people here who had intel from the base of the terrorists," he explained to the lady.

"Are you sure those three aren't working with the enemy?"

"They work as vigilantes who warn the police about any suspicious behavior."

"Okay, they'll be there in thirty minutes. Stand by until they arrive," she announced as the radio fell completely silent.

"Alright, do you guys wanna wait inside? I'm pretty sure you're here to help, right?" He offered as he held the door for them.

"I didn't think cops were allowed to do that," Paul replied.

"When you bring information like that, be prepared to show what side you're on. It doesn't matter if I trust you guys, if the other officers don't like you, they'll throw you in jail. This city is corrupt, and sadly nobody notices that buildings are being torn down with people inside of them. Police are doing this and yet they say they serve and protect," the man complained.

Suddenly, the ground began to rumble as shouts were heard in the distance. Paul and his allies all turned around abruptly to see where the rumbling could be coming from. They didn't see anything but a street that had very few cars starting their days.

"What is that?" Sean asked.

"I don't know, leader, you tell me?" Gwen snarled.

"Is there a reason why you're picking on Sean?" Paul asked.

"Well," Gwen defnded. "I just wanna see if he can toughen out, I mean the dudes a coward."

"True," Paul agreed.

"Hey, I'm not a coward," Sean squeaked, making the two giggle like kids.

The sun that was arising was beginning to be shut out by something enormous. The four looked upwards to the sky to see an enemy pirate ship flying through the air. Painted red and black, Paul knew who this was.

"The day is becoming night due to that big ass ship, do you think it's after us?" Sean asked.

"Dude, they're not here for the cops or any civilians, not even you." Paul panicked as he stared in fear at the large boat in the sky. "They're after us," he cautioned as he grabbed Gwen by the wrist, dragging her past the guard into the courthouse.

Sean rushed in behind the two with his weapon holstered on his back as it bounced.

"What's the plan Sean?" Paul asked as they entered the lobby.

They stood there in an empty and vast lobby, where a single chandelier hung from the ceiling.

"Where are the metal detectors, and the seats for officers?" Sean asked as they stood under the chandelier.

"The metal detectors were implanted into the doors, if it went off we'd have gotten shot. Is this sword not made of metal or something Gwen?" Paul asked as he approached the stairs in front of them.

"No, it's not made of metal. It's made from plants, minerals, and rocks in the ground. I tightly squeezed a grappling hook into the handle for a better escape," she explained as she followed Paul up the stairs.

"Wait," Sean muffled from under his mask as he trailed behind. "First off," he urged as the couple stopped walking and turned around. "Are we just going to leave the militia to do all the work? We're supposed to protect this city."

"You're right," Paul began. "Basically, our side objective is to protect these people, but our main mission is to be alive when Byron and the lady come back. If you want us to, we could turn around and struggle like those militias out there, or we could continue to our main objective and fight when necessary. Listen," Paul began as he stepped down a step to be face to face with Bull. "I'm talking to you as Bison when I say we don't want to be dead before our allies regroup with us. As a leader, you're not to put your heart into the decisions you make, but look at the situation at hand.

"What's more important in an example where there are millions of lives at stake but doing our objective is a need because if we don't the entire omni-verse could be in shambles or destroyed. Risking millions is better than risking uncountable numbers. No, it won't be an easy choice, I understand. When you left the house, I had to become my own leader. I realized that the way I was living wasn't at all normal. Lying to stay out of trouble, putting the blame against my own sibling, lying for the wrong person. Do you know what drove me and you both back there? I'll tell you, it was fear, the one feeling we cannot let ourselves get overwhelmed by again," he concluded as he turned around and began to walk up the stairs.

"Alright," Bull agreed as they rushed up the fifty flights of stairs.

The ground shook and the building felt as if it were to tumble beneath their feet as they reached the door to the roof. Bison and Gwen stepped aside to let Bull ramm his arm through the door like a bullet.

They walked to the edge of the roof to look down on all of the chaos that ensued below.

"Damn," Bull began. "So, logically speaking, this is our new reality. It's hard to understand, but I finally get it. We have to be the ones who lay down our lives to save infinite lives. We have to be willing to fight for days on end just because we want to call ourselves protectors. For what, they may ask," he rambled as he stared down. "Maybe because we're insane, or maybe it's because our normal lives were intruded by a charade of bullshit and it dragged us in. There's so much to think about," Bull ended as Bison began.

"I understand," he nodded as he stood next to Bull, where Gwen was on his right. "It'll take a few days to actually understand why, but that doesn't matter right now. What matters is that," he stated, pointing at a taxi speeding towards them.

Gwen began to inspect her surroundings as she looked straight, right, left, at the rooftops, at the ground. Then, her attention shot back to her left to a rooftop where a man was holding what seemed to be a tube.

"Rocket!" Gwen yelled as the tube made a whistle sound. She followed it's trajectory, noticing that it was headed towards the taxi. "Impact," Gwen shouted as she slipped off of the building, letting gravity drop her.

"We're not going to survive that," Bull and Bison announced in harmony.

"Trust yourselves," Gwen yelled as her voice disappeared.

"Shit," Bull began. "Do you know how to slide down a building?" he asked as he looked down to see Gwen pressed against the building.

"That's it," Bison concluded as he pulled out his sword. "We've gotta soften our landing with the force we use from the fall against the wall,"

"What?" Bull asked, stunned for a second. "Oh!" he jolted in realization. "You mean we can soften our landing by grabbing onto the wall, slowing ourselves down?"

"Yup," Bison agreed as he let himself fall. He free fell for quite a few floors before he stabbed his sword against the building, barely hitting the ground. Yanking him downwards as it suddenly stopped, he looked above himself to see Bull stab his gun into the wall.

"Good job," he congratulated as he looked up.

"Thanks, but what now?" Bull asked.

"Figure it out," Bison replied as he jumped onto the ground and rushed to the now flipped over taxi.

"I got it," Bull thought as he let himself fall five floors to the ground. "If I have to protect my family, then I'm going to need to tap into my bloodlust," he thought as he began to breathe air into his nose, releasing it from his mouth slowly. "I'll defend them with my gun, attacking anyone who gets close."

Bison began to catch up to Gwen, who was running almost as fast as light. She turned her head to look at Bison as she ran and began to talk.

"Your natural speed must be high!" she yelled in shock as they approached the taxi.

Bison ran to the left side while Gwen ran to the right as bullets and explosives were seen flying through the entire city. Tanks shot craters into demons, completely ignoring the metal from their blades. They did their best to avoid the five as the rescue persisted with Gwen grabbing Byron and Bison grabbing the lady in a pink shirt. They hoisted them onto their shoulders and looked at each other.

"Let's get back to the building, make sure everybody gets inside of the building," Gwen instructed Bison as they met up at the front of the flipped over taxi.

He nodded as they began to run. They climbed broken cars and began to jump from broken car to broken car as tank missiles flew past their faces.

"Bull, let's go," Bison commanded as he ran past the man shooting down every enemy that almost caught the two.

"Right," he nodded as he turned around. He immediately stopped in his tracks when he saw four brute demons standing with their fists ready to brawl. The middle one landed a swift right blow to the cheek of Bull, causing him to fly backwards into another group of brute demons.

Gwen and Bison ran past the tanks and army men shooting, blasting through the glass doors almost breaking them.

"Where's Bull?" Bison asked as they gently laid the two on the cold, shiny marble floor.

"He's not here, he must be stuck," Gwen replied.

"I'm going back," Bison pressured as he stood to his feet, turning to place his hand onto the door handle. He stopped his movement when he heard Gwen's voice.

"Don't get yourself killed, Bison, or we're all dead," she worried as she lifted her mask to reveal her face, giving him a comforting smile. One that made him want to sleep as she put her mask back down.

He hesitated a moment, still staring at Gwen before he bolted out of the doors towards Bull. He was seen to be getting pummeled by about nine brutes, he was surrounded. Running past the army men and tanks, he pulled out his sword and extended it to the right of him. Keeping the blade away as he ran, his eyes turned crimson as he approached the group. He went to the left of the group, stabbing his blade into the back of the demon on the furthest left, disabling its kidney.

He then pulled his sword out of the demon's back, ripping its kidney from its slot. He aimed towards the demon on the right, swinging his sword into the back of its neck. He snapped it, instantly killing the creature. He then jumped over Bull as he pulled his sword from the neck and slit into the throat of the demon across from him piercing through its neck, the demon fell onto its back with a thump as Bison's sword was still in its throat.

He sat atop the demon as he took time to think while a demon was swinging a fist from the left. "That's two," he thought as it seemed like time slowed down before placing his sword onto the wrist of the demon.

He twisted the blade around its wrist, slicing it off as Bison used the momentum and threw himself foot first into the demon's face, causing it to fly away from the group.

"I can't take them all out, I'll retrieve Bull and leave," he thought as he grabbed Bull when he landed. He dragged him by the shoulder to get him closer to himself.

"I know what it's like brother, it hurts even me when it happens," he whispered as he lifted the heavy Bull onto his back..

He then pushed past the two brutes he originally injured, charging towards the radio station.

He ran about twenty feet before a demon hammer was seen flying throughout the air, right towards Bison. He looked to his left, down the broken and shattered road, to see a huge hammer hit him in the face. He got carried to the right as the hammer was still flying. Bull was seen to be tossed ahead, not too far in front of Bison.

Gwen opened up the door to further inspect the situation as to why it was taking so long to recover Bull. To her surprise, she saw a flood of demons collecting into one location to the left of her current position. In closer inspection, she saw Bison and Bull, both motionless and lying on the ground waiting to be killed by the demons.

"Bison!" She screamed as she ran outside towards their direction. Her feet could barely keep up with her mind as she almost tripped several times, reaching them in less than a second.

She pulled a purple stick from behind her back as she crouched in front of the two, guarding them with a barrier. The demons of all sizes, small, medium and large, began to swarm the three on all sides as Gwen's hair began to rise and her aura projected a severely dark purple tint.

"Do you want to fight your queen, servants?" She asked as the demons froze in place.

A demon that stood eight feet and wore a black cult coat appeared from the crowd, standing in front of the army.

"I am Satan's first in command, the demon he holds responsible for the bounties I retrieve. My name is Bartho, and if you must queen, please stand aside. This matter does not concern you," he warned as he unsheathed a hammer from his back.

"I do not care," she snapped with uncertainty in her voice. "These men do not concern you. If you are looking for Paul, he isn't on this Earth for we transferred him unto another one. What you are doing here is completely unacceptable by peace terms. Leave and find him elsewhere," she commanded in confidence.

"Don't lie to me like that," Bartho spat as he gave Gwen a dirty look. "We know the man behind you is the true Paul, and we want him dead."

"For what?" She asked.

"Being Satan's daughter, you would know that removing a demon from their resting place too early is completely unallowed. Also, queen, you could be put up to trial for harboring a refugee, or for bringing a mere mortal to the underworld. So if you must, please back down."

"Never," she pressed as she lunged at the demon with her staff, stabbing him in the chest.

The demon gave a bellowing laugh, creating an echo as he let his head fall back. The army stood, waiting and watching as the demon silenced himself and began to talk.

"Did you think that would work?" Bartho asked as he grimly smiled.

Suddenly, her staff began to glow as the light around them began to fade, turning the entire area around them gray for a mere moment. A blast was released from her staff, causing any human eardrums to explode as the blast covered about a forest worth of land. The buildings around them crumbled as people ran towards the exit of Skylark trying to evacuate.

When the smoke settled, the entire area in front of Gwen was gone, as if an artist erased a chunk of the Earth beneath them. The lava began to flow as the Earth caved inwards. Gwen fell to her knees as the staff fell to her side, making her go limp.

Bison began to regain consciousness as he rubbed his head, groaning in pain. He looked towards the beaten and dried out Gwen and ran to her side.

"What happened?" He asked as he let her fall back into his arms.

She looked up to him and weakly stated, "If I hadn't done it, we would be dead."

"Not that," he ignored as he picked her up onto his shoulder. "Why were you on your knees?" He asked as demons began to approach him from the west and north.

"I used all of my energy to blow away that scum demon, cocky bitch." She taunted weakly.

Bison walked over to the still unconscious Bull and hooked him under his armpit as he ran through the demons, barreling through the heavy muscle as they tried to grab them. They pushed until they reached the steps to the courthouse, crumbling as he was unable to climb the steps. He gritted his teeth and began to think,

"They're just lousy steps, why can't I move," he thought as he looked onto the ground, seeing a pool of blood to his right.

Suddenly, a hand dragged their unconscious bodies into the courtroom building,

They sat in the cold air while the army outside held off the very few demons left. Gwen was lying next to a bloody Bison, who was lying next to Bull.

"Someone's bleeding," Byron mentioned from the blood on the floor.

The woman began to walk towards each person, inspecting their clothing and bodies for wounds.

"On the exterior," she began as she observed Gwen. "Did not seem harmed when I dragged them in, but of course everybody misses something." She stated as she observed Bison, stopping to stare at a little red spot on the back of his neck.

"What's that?" Byron asked as she turned Bison's head gently, gasping when she saw what it was.

"He was shot in the neck, it looks like it punctured through but didn't pass completely through. And if you think about it," she observed as she flipped Bison onto his back, then back over. "Bison is a battle mindset, meaning he would do anything and everything to win a battle or to complete the mission he is assigned. Even getting shot in the neck wouldn't affect Bison, but if Paul were to awaken, he would probably die due to the lack of ki," she explained as Gwen sat up, looking to her left to see the bloody Bison.

"Move," Gwen shouted, motherlike, as she pushed the woman out of the way.

"What are you…" she began as Gwen reached for her bookbag.

"Where's my bookbag?" She asked, annoyed.

"Here," Byron offered as she looked up to see him holding her bag.

"She thanked him before yanking the bag from his hand, putting a single strap onto her shoulder.

She reached down and put her arm behind Bison's head, and her other one under his hip. She carried him to a receptionist desk not too far away, gently laying him onto his back. Gwen then put her book bag next to him, across from her as she stood on the right of the table.

Rummaging through her belongings, she pulled out a pair of scissors, a scalpel, a pair of tweezers, rubbing alcohol, and a magnifying glass. Byron, the woman, and now the awake Bull, crowded around her as she untied his mask, gently lifting it from his face before placing it next to her bag.

"My youngest brother?" Byron asked in shock.

"Yeah, did you think you were fighting with strangers?" The woman replied.

"Well, actually," he pondered for a minute as Gwen gently placed the tip of her tweezers inside of Bison's neck, going deeper to find the bullet. "Yes, I thought that maybe I could find better people."

"You guys don't like Paul, do y'all?" Gwen asked with a snarl as she gently pulled the tweezers out of his neck. "Yeah, he might not have done some things you guys would accept, but he tries based on his situation. Instead of misunderstanding someone, take the time to understand their psychi." She began to cut off the shirt with her small scissors. "Without knowing yourself, also, can be another reason why you don't understand people. You have nothing to reflect upon to learn and develop."

"Yeah, but Paul couldn't understand us if he tried."

Turning around, stopping her procedure, she began to fuss.

"Tell me, if you were in a pile of confusion and chaos, what would you think within that situation? A human mind bends to their situations and upbringing. If you had a conversation with this man, he'd understand y'all more than you guys could understand a dictionary. The reason being is that everybody badgered Paul, and in turn, it made him look into the mirror to find every flaw within himself before caring about others. So look in the mirror and shut up as I finish," she finished as she turned around, continuing her operation.

"She has a point," Bull agreed as he untied his mask, letting it drop into his right hand. "But the bigger question at hand is what we're going to do about the principle. For all we know, he could be making an escape."

"Correct," the woman agreed as she stood next to Sean. "If we attempt to make a slow ambush, he could move onto the next multiverse. In doing that, we would have to chase him until we've caught up to them."

"Wait, doesn't that mean we would be going from universe, to another alternate universe, saving that universe after saving this one just to catch a puss on the run?" Bull asked, trying to wrap his head around the situation.

"If you could understand what you just said, yes. In simpler terms," the woman began as she snapped her fingers.

She was engulfed in pink smoke, making her completely disappear. When the smoke cleared, she was wearing her yellow dress and held her staff. She waved the staff behind her and created a chalkboard out of thin air.

"When Mr Scorch escapes to this universe's alternate reality, he'll be entering into a different galaxy. Yes, you four may travel freely through realities at will. You must be able to if anything like this were to take place again. I think Paul may already know this, it's easy for him to figure things out by a few words," she concluded, turning her attention towards Gwen who was still performing surgery.

She turned to look at Sean and Byron as they sat in folding chairs they found propped up just a few feet away from the operating table. They sat a yard from the table as they stared in amazement.

"Anyway, when he runs to a different reality, he might try to trigger something to slow you down. Most enemies will, but you cannot keep everyone back to take care of an issue. If the man or woman keeps running, send one or two protectors to chase them down before they cause anymore chaos.

"I'm not going to be here all of the time, but I will be watching with my husband from above. For I am the High Priestess, and the High Priest is my husband. Unfortunately for you guys, this is just a trial run. When this omniverse is secured, you will be placed into a vigorous training held by a higher being," she concluded as she gently placed her chalk onto the metal.

"If you're the High Priestess," Byron began as he stood to his feet. "What's your natural talent?" He asked boldly as they stood up from their chairs.

She inhaled a deep breath into her nose, releasing it slowly from her mouth before speaking.

"If you must know, I am willing to tell you for the sake of trusting me. Not all humans are the smartest, but you four are the smartest beings on this Earth. My natural talent is the ability to teach well and care for my underlings as if they were one of my own. My protection is almost as strong as my husband's, but he can expand his natural talent to an extent I hate to see," she mumbled as she stared at the ground.

"What's to be upset about?" Gwen asked as she wiped her hands on a bloody towel. "My natural talent is only to call a hideout by eyesight. Yours is to help put those up to the task of protecting and not dying. If anything you're better than anyone, other than Paul, that's a good soul. I don't like Byron's face, and I just flat out hate Sean," she opinionated as she put the towel down and leaned her body against the table.

"The last crew I taught was killed mercilessly by Satin an odd seventeen years ago. Though one survived, it took this long for anyone to do anything about the protectors disappearing. Apparently, Satin raped the woman protector. So me and the High Priest talked to Cerberus, but we were not allowed in. It hurts us to know we let that happen, but we won't let it happen again because you guys will prevail," she emphasized with hope as she stared at Bull, then Byron, then Gwen, and finally to the unconscious Paul.

"You four are my multiverse warriors, and no matter what, you will prevail and live on. For if you die, the circle is going to keep spinning. Do not fail us, nor the creator for he's entrusting you four to protect what he has wonderfully built. We are the ones who appreciate in the midst of those who are unappreciative," she lectured as she stood straight.

"Right," they all harmonized, except for Paul, as they stood straight.

"One question," Gwen began as she checked on Paul. "How aren't there any demons busting into the courthouse right now?" She asked.

"Well, if you look out of the window, you'll see that there are demons about to break in. With time being stopped as soon as I snapped my fingers. Not only did you have time to finish your procedure, but I also had time to lecture you all," the woman explained.

"How long can you stop time for?" Sean asked as he walked up to the door, peeling the curtain away from the window.

What he saw horrified him as an axe was seen to be poking into the window. The military were nowhere to be found amongst the ocean of demons.

"I can stop it for as long as I'd like, me and my husband cannot be beaten in battle. However, if we do fight anyone of equal power, existence will no longer exist. The creator would have to start all over and erase both me and my husband," the woman explained.

"We better get a move on then," Sean commanded as he let the curtain fall, walking back to the group.

"There's a helicopter on the roof to take us to our destination. My time stop may be infinite, but using it for our own selfish desires is forbidden. There's only a select few moments we can slip past without being noticed. Also, my time stop doesn't just stop what's in this universe, but what's in this omniverse. It's because of a release of my high energy through the air, spreading faster than light," she rambled.

"All right," Gwen finished as she stowed her items away in her bag, strapping it around her shoulders. "You said all of his wounds were healed?" She asked as she inspected his neck.

"Well, the surgery you did was all yours. Any small fractures or broken bones any of you had is healed. However, Bison himself can take insane amounts of damage. I mean, a hammer to the face should've knocked his clock off of the wall, if you know what I mean. That, and he had a bullet in his neck at the moment of impact. When I inspected him, the wound was deep enough to at least touch his spine. It wasn't a regular bullet either, so it had to be a sniper," she rambled as they all stared at her.

"Was I rambling again?" She asked, embarrassed.

"No, not at all," Gwen replied sarcastically as they turned towards the stairs.

"Everyone, put on your masks. We've gotta get going before time starts and we're surrounded in a sea of despair." Sean commanded as he stood at the base of the stairs, holding his gun diagonal on his chest. "The mission is to evacuate and take out the source at all costs, except our lives. If you need help, seek an ally because things could get tricky."

He turned around and began to run up the stairs with Paul on Gwen's shoulder, bouncing like he was a sack of potatoes.

"I'm going to start time," the High Priestess initiated halfway up the staircase.

Their legs were heavy and their hearts slowed for a moment as the air shifted around them. Bringing a strong energy to a center, then releasing it throughout the air. The sound of rumbling was heard as they sprinted up the stairs and the entire building shook beneath their feet.

"We've gotta hurry," Gwen stated as she rushed past the leader, Bull.

"These stairs aren't easy, if you had human legs you'd understand," he tried explaining.

"I'm holding a probably one hundred thirty pound man, as a woman, and I'm burning your heels," Gwen angrily snapped.

"Relax Gwen," the High Priestess calmly instructed. "Anger will only confuse and blind you. Think it through thoroughly, do you want to rush and cause an entire mishap?" She asked.

"Damnit," Gwen thought as she gritted her teeth. "I can't even be mad because she's right. Who is she? She's really smart on a lot of topics, probably smarter than me if I show it. How smart is Paul?" She pondered as they reached the broken rooftop door, hearing the sound of helicopter blades.

They piled through the opening in a single file line as they rushed towards the helicopter. Bull slipped in first, claiming the seat on the upper left. Gwen laid Paul in the middle of the two seats and sat at the upper right of the helicopter. As the High Priestess climbed into the helicopter, the building began to shake.

It wasn't just the building Byron realized as he stared across the town. The sight of creatures emerging from the ground paralyzed Byron as his worst fears came to life.

Realizing that Byron froze, Bull turned around to look across the city to see the creatures emerge.

"It's begun," the High Priestess horrifically blurted as she stared in fear at the city being consumed by undead humans.

Witches, kings, knights, and everything that once walked the Earth arose from the ground as the city was enveloped into a dark storm.

"Byron, get in!" Bull yelled, but it was useless. He was stunned by the reality that crashed into him, like a meteor to the Earth's surface.

Suddenly, the building began to shake uncontrollably, causing the foundation to crack.

"The building's going to collapse," Gwen informed as she began to climb out of the helicopter towards Byron.

Bison regained consciousness and stopped her from moving, sitting her back down. He jumped out of the helicopter to run towards Byron as Gwen tried to reason with him. She attempted to yank and keep him in the helicopter. It was useless because when Bison's toe touched the building, it collapsed underneath him.

The building crumbled as the helicopter remained airborne, making Byron and Bison crumble into a pit of demons and falling debris

"Nooo!" Gwen yelled as the High Priestess held her from jumping out.

"Remember, two people go one way and the other go another. We're going to need to go with that plan for now, if we go back, Scorch will escape."

"There's three of us, use your power to kill him, I don't care. I want to go back," she complained as she attempted to break herself from the woman's surprisingly strong arms.

"If I fight him, the entire omni-verse could be destroyed causing a collapse of good and evil," she tried reasoning.

"Why are you so strong?" Gwen asked as she calmed down and sat down in her seat. Her mind raced with thoughts as she tried to contact Bison through telekinesis.

"He must be unconscious," she thought as she stopped trying.

"It's Paul, if he needs to survive, he will." Bull reassured Gwen.

"Alright, to the mansion then," the High Priestess commanded with doubt in her voice as the helicopter flew off into the distance over the dark horizon.

Chapter 12

The survival test

The man without a mask awoke in the middle of a crowd filled with demons and undead. A man emerged from a crowd wearing a dark, almost black, red Priest outfit. His face was beautiful, like a man carved out of pure desire.

"Hello Byron," he spoke in a low voice.

Byron looked around to see little to no room to move. Bison, the man in the red mask, laid face down on the ground next to him in a pool of what seemed to be his own blood.

"Who are you?" Byron trembled with intense fear in his voice.

"Since I haven't introduced myself yet. I am the Low Priest, and I'm here to ask you a few questions," the Low Priest introduced himself as he stood mere inches from Byron. "What's your natural talent, my boy?" He asked.

"I don't know, " he shuddered.

"Hmm, let's strike a deal," he proposed as he sat in front of Byron, crossing his legs.

"You have too much power to be unnoticeable, how are you here?" Byron asked.

"Since there is an abundance of evil in this area, it's pretty easy to mask my aura. You, however, are different. Your brothers, Bull and Bison, were meant to protect the omni-verses. You," he convinced as he placed a finger onto Byron's chest. "Are meant to destroy everything and stop them. It is in your destiny." He alluded as he placed his hand back onto his own lap.

"They're my brothers, a prophecy can't pit me against family. It's against the rules," he contested.

"True, but they're not your brothers because I am your father. You are meant to serve me. Who says you three are actually related, I mean you did split up when you were younger. You were the only one alone. Why weren't Paul and Sean placed in the same home as you?" He questioned.

"But you can't be my father, a being of higher existence can't possess earthly kids," Byron argued back.

"The creator has infinite children he's created, such as the High Priest and I. I had intercourse with a woman I stole from the omniverse, actually, the universe we stand in. She bared a child that was given to a family that couldn't support their own, causing you and your current 'brothers' to form as a so-called family. They're all you knew when you were a kid before you were split up, I understand, but Dad's here to make it all better.

"I have made many deals with the true devil himself, all of these enemies are under my command. Suppose I make you my right hand and I would give you all of the power you'd ever need. Bison, the multiverse protector, would be weaker than you. So son, are you in?" He bargained as he offered his hand.

He absorbed the information carefully, reaching his hand out cautiously as he accepted the words he uttered. Bison began to stir as he turned onto his back, looking to his right through the holes in his mask.

"What's going on?" Bison asked as their hands connected, sending a shockwave of energy throughout the ruined city.

They stood to their feet, side by side as they turned around and disappeared into the crowd of enemies.

"BYRON!" Bison screamed as the enemies stared at him like they haven't eaten in days. He reached to his side for his sword, but it was gone. "Shit," he mumbled as he stood to his feet and put his fists up. "I'm so fucked," he whispered under his breathe as the enemies closed in on him.

"Do you think he's okay?" Gwen asked as the helicopter landed on a remote island far from Skylark.

The island was inhabited by animals of every variety with a humongous castle surrounded by forest on the edge. It was nice and unkempt as they landed next to the castle in a clear field.

"I'm pretty sure Bison will protect himself and Byron. He's a fighter meant to serve the High Priest, he's going to be fine." Bull confidently assured as he jumped off of the side of the helicopter.

"Has he gotten bigger?" Gwen asked the High Priestess, who's eyes were closed. "What's wrong?" She asked.

"This isn't right," the High Priestess pondered as her eyes burst open, showing obvious fear.

Sending shivers down both of their spines, Gwen and Bull focused their attention on the Priestess.

"What's wrong?" Bull asked as she hunched over with her head on her knees.

"This was a mistake, I didn't think he would come so soon," she muttered repeatedly.

"Priestess, what happened?" Gwen asked as she shook her shoulder.

"Bisons at his wits end, the Low Priest was here," she trembled.

"Was?" Bull echoed.

"What're you saying? Spit it out!" Gwen pleaded with worry in her voice.

"He's going to be traumatized, he's alone. We need to go back to town," The Priestess pleaded with the pilot.

"We're out of gas, the only way we can go anywhere is teleportation," the pilot concluded.

"Then let's pray that the Creator has mercy on his soul," the Priestess agonized.

"If you ever need to get atop of a roof, use this," Bison thought as he flashbacked to Gwen handing him a handgun. "Keep it where there's a hole for a gun," she instructed as she shoved it into his hand.

"What is it?" he asked as he accepted the gift, reaching behind him and strapping it into the hole.

"A grappling hook," Gwen concluded as she faded from his mind.

He laid there, motionless as demons pummeled him and zombies began to start chewing his left arm. His energy was depleted for he could only take out one hundred demons and undead alike with only his bare hands. He reached behind him as he felt a pain in his hip, as if he were laying on something. He pulled out the pistol and shot it into the air, letting his arm go as he faded away.

"I keep losing signal," Gwen complained as they stormed the beautiful maze of a castle, running around corners and into dead ends.

"He's alone, I don't expect him to survive a sea of enemies. How could Byron betray us?" Bull angrily asked.

"The Low Priests' natural talent is persuasion. He could convince you that you're a species of animal that nobody's ever heard of. Combine that with Byron's natural talent, and there's nothing we can do," the Priestess explained as they delved deeper and deeper into the wild hallways.

"So what you're saying is that the Low Priest can brainwash you hardcore, and you'll never know. Right?" Gwen asked as she led the group.

"Exactly, and since we are here, Scorchs natural talent is intellect far greater than any deity's intellect. In turn, this is what happened. If he can hop dimensions to get to the other universes, or omni-verses I should say, we're going to need to chase him," The Priestess explained.

"If I have this right, you're telling us that universes are just other timelines making other universes?" Bull asked, confused.

"No, I mean that the space and time between the universes could be multiple timelines in the dimensions leading to a singular universe, causing an alternate universe to the universe just a space jump away," she tried explaining more.

"What exactly is a dimension?" Bull asked.

"It's the space between the universes, basically the gap between two universes. There are multiple dimensions at play, considering that dimensions get more dangerous when you travel through the omni-verse's dimensions instead of the universal dimensions. The further out into space you go, like from universe to multiverse, the more dangerous space becomes.

"My heads gonna explode," Bull concluded as he almost tripped.

"Keep your head together," Gwen insisted as she outran the two. "We have to stop Scorch and save Bison no matter the cost. If we aren't one as we are, then who's going to protect the multiple universes that exist? Let's go," she commanded as she ran faster.

A man wearing a mask was seen hanging up high from a building, his one arm was raised as if he were holding something. He stirred, looking upwards to see his hand stitched into the handle.

"So, Gwen does care," he thought weakly as he used the gun's rope to pull himself onto the rooftop. His arms and legs were beyond repair as his body ached with bites and cuts. "Bison," the man thought as he closed his eyes, entering into his imagination.

He stood in a pitch black field of darkness as he bravely stared into the abyss. A wounded man was seen to appear from the darkness, just enough for the man to see him.

"Is this all we have to offer?" He asked the man.

"Your body cannot take much more. If you do, you will die Paul." The man spoke in a low tone.

"Come on Bison, you're my battle mindset. You're supposed to be able to handle this," he argued.

"And what about you Paul? I can't just carry the load while you sit back and sleep. This was the problem with Lucyfer, you never knew when to stand up to her. You're weak," he exclaimed.

Paul dropped his eyes downwards to his feet as he pondered.

"Alright, maybe you're right. Maybe being a kid scared…"

"Don't give me that sympathy bullshit. You and I both know that you're too scared to let out your true self. You were so scared that you literally lost yourself and split it away from your soul, letting it rot away. You and I both know that if the roles were reversed, we wouldn't be in this mess," Bison contested.

"All I've ever wanted to do was protect those weaker than me because if not me then who? If we don't put our lives on the line to save those who cannot save themselves, then who will?" Paul argued.

"Then use that to help me, we're in this because you have doubts that are holding me back. I follow you because I am you, but I am a humbled you. I am a you that can see through anyone's sarcastic remark. I am a you that could conquer omni-verses time and time again without failure, but I bow to a coward," he mocked.

"You don't bow to a coward, I am just the man who doesn't seek senseless murdering. I'd rather seek protection than let anyone stain my hands with innocent blood," Paul angrily stated.

"So, you do kill?" Bison asked.

"The only reason I would see killing in a sense of good is when it's a scummy enemy."

"So, like Mr Scorch and how he wanted to give us all of the power," Bison mocked as he waved his hands around and laughed.

Paul began to laugh as well as he talked through the laughter.

"Did you hear when he said, 'You could be my right hand,'" he mocked as well. "As if neither me nor you would be caught under someone's thumb again."

"You've got that right," Bison agreed as the darkness around them faded, revealing a room with no doors or windows.

"So, what about the problem at hand?" Paul asked as he leaned against a wall.

"Do you have a joint?" Bison asked as he leaned beside him.

"In this head, we have everything," he responded as he pulled out a rolled piece of paper and lit the tip. He took a pull as the smoke began to circle them both. They passed it back and forth while they talked.

"So, Byron's betrayed us." Bison broke the silence as he took a pull from the joint, releasing a cough as the smoke escaped his mouth.

"True, but that doesn't mean he's going to stay that way. We can always talk,"

"Or beat," Bison intruded as he handed Paul the joint.

"Yes, or beat him back onto our side. Aren't we going to get affected by the zombies that bit us? I kind of felt something earlier."

"Well, our friend Gwen injected something into us after the surgery. It might have something to do with this current situation. If I am correct, she also injected the others with the same needle."

"How do you know this?" He asked as they dropped the empty, burnt paper, onto the floor.

"I don't die when you do, causing you to be immune to most things since I'm technically not alive. What I'm saying is, I am a soul that was created through another soul, but I do not invade, I simply live by your side. I have no true purpose but to fight, I am your will to live."

"Well, that makes a lot of sense now," Paul mumbled as the room began to fade.

"Are we waking up?" Bison asked.

"Yeah, and it seems like I'll be in control. I'll fight for us, I promise," Paul chippered as he gave him a thumbs up before disappearing.

Gasping, the man awoke to life like a dead man.

"Odd theory," he thought as he dragged himself to a generator, sitting his back against the cool metal. "What if the syringe Bison mentioned neutralized the turning process," he pondered as he looked over the horizon. "Is this the only building left?" He asked himself as he stumbled to his feet.

The air was moist and thick with humidity as Paul looked down onto the city not too far below himself to see the buildings sunken into the ground. The sky was covered by a red, misty cloud.

"So, you survived?" A familiar voice from behind taunted, shaking Paul to his core.

"You did not," Paul gritted as his voice and face turned into hatred.

They stood in front of a humongous castle dual door littered with gems. Two lion faces were seen on each door, it was the entrance to the throne room.

"So, who wants to go first?" Bull asked as he let his rifle rest on his shoulder.

"You of course," The Priestess bantered as she signaled him to open the door with her staff.

Gwen stood behind them with her eyes closed, attempting to connect with Paul.

"Come on," she struggled as she thought. "Paul, just give me a signal," she mumbled as she wandered through the little brain waves left on the Earth. She was about to give up until she felt a similar yet weak brain wave.

"Paul," she thought in excitement as someone tapped her shoulder twice, causing her to lose the connection.

"We don't have much time," the Priestess informed with her staff extended.

With sorrow, she arose and followed behind the large man and woman. Being greeted by darkness all around, the walls were invisible as the doors suddenly shut behind them. Gwen turned around to attempt to pry open the door, but there was nothing behind her.

"What the hell?" She questioned as she looked around the dark room.

"We're in a trap," the Priestess acknowledged as they stood in the room. "Let me brighten things up," she joked as she raised her staff. A bright light began to illuminate brightly throughout the room, as if it were daylight, exposing rotting corpses of knights and royals.

They walked down the creepy aisle towards the throne chair as the floor creaked with every step. Bull led the group towards the throne as the light showed spiderwebs covering the corners of the walls, as if it were abandoned.

"Look, a note," he pointed as he approached the throne chair. He picked up the note and read it aloud, "If you are reading this Bison, I want to face you personally in the galaxy parallel to this galaxy. If you need a compass, I'll leave one that will lead you to my destination. Even in space it won't lose connection. If anyone but you pursues me, I will set traps within a few galaxies, infecting them with undead."

"So what you're saying is," Gwen snarled as she snatched the note from Bull. "Scorch had a run in with Bison, tasted his power, and wants to die? And if we try to pursue he'll infect any or all of the universes? Coward," she mumbled as she wrinkled the paper and threw it away.

"What's the obsession with Bison anyway?" The Priestess asked as she picked up a compass sitting on the arm of the chair. She handed it to Gwen who stowed it into her pink bookbag.

"He's a living, breathing soul within a body that we believe created it. Anyone with that much mental strength could possibly be of use to the wrong person. Let's just hope Scorch isn't as mentally strong," Gwen pondered as they looked around the room.

"Why'd you do it?" Paul asked as they stood on opposite sides of the roof.

The wind violently blew across the rooftop as the ashes from the city flew across the air.

"The Low Priest ordered me to kill you because of your mental strength. He says your body is weak but your mind can overcome what your body is subdued to," Byron began.

"You left me to die, but we're brothers. We aren't meant to fight at the end of the day. I'm always going to have your back whether you feed me to a horde or not. Don't let the Low Priest confuse you, for what he's told you was nothing but lies," Bison argued as he shifted his body.

"Lies!" Byron exclaimed. "The Low Priest knows of the sins of The Creator, and we will kill anyone in our path."

"Don't make me do this," Paul pleaded as Byron lunged towards him with his forearm in front his face.

Paul ran forward with his right forearm facing Byron as they clashed. They stood face to face as Paul was obviously out of energy.

"You're weak, just give up," Byron challenged.

"There's no such thing as being weak," Paul backfired.

They pushed away from each other with a shove that made them almost fall on their ass.

"The demons and undead were munching on your flesh, you've got no energy," Byron mocked as he suddenly appeared in front of Paul.

He swung out his hand in a semi circle in front of him, sending out a strong shockwave of wind that blasted Paul off of the rooftop. As he fell, he tried to grab onto something to cushion his landing, but it was useless.

The enemies on the ground stared at Paul as he fell, waiting to make him into dinner. Byron appeared in front of Paul and kicked him into the building, causing the structure to bend.

He coughed blood into his hand as he laid on the rugged carpet, his arms and legs were practically useless.

"How did you get so strong?" Paul asked as he sat up, supporting himself on a chair.

"My father gave me a quarter of his power. It's not much, however, it will be enough to kill you in your early stage," Byron responded as he teleported a straight right punch at Paul.

In response, Paul tilted his head to the left, grabbing Byron's legs with his feet. Tumbling, Byron fell to the ground with a thump. His face hit a chair that supported Paul's back, causing blood to leak from his forehead. Paul twisted his body to put Byron in a leg lock as they laid straight with legs intertwined.

"Why brother?" Paul begged for answers.

"We were never brothers," Byron responded on his stomach as he twisted himself out of the leg lock, breaking Paul's right leg.

He howled in pain as his shin was misplaced, making his blood pour onto the carpet like a leaking pipe. Paul dragged himself backwards, towards the hole they've made into the building. Byron stood to his feet with brutality in his eyes.

"I want you dead," Byron mocked as a bright light illuminated his hand.

Paul looked at Byron in the eyes with sadness and despair, causing Byron to feel sympathy. Paul spun onto his hands, standing on them as he twisted his hands around super fast. Using his body weight and the spin force, he threw himself at Byron.

Knocking him off of his feet, Paul landed onto his chest as he pinned his arms down. The energy blast flew into the ceiling behind Paul, causing the portion affected to collapse and almost break Paul's left foot.

"I'm not trying to hurt you brother," Paul begged yet again for Byron to wake up. "Can't you see that he's lying to you Byron. If I don't have you I'd be begging The Creator for you back, we're family. This is not supposed to happen brother, just listen to me. Sean and I fought all of the time," he pleaded as he stared Byron in the eyes.

"Stop your lies. Father told me you would try this. I am…" Byron began as his head was slammed into the ground.

"You're going to listen," he argued with mercy in his heart. "We don't know our parents, we were taken at a young age and put into an adoption agency. Any guy could walk up to you and claim to be your father, but it's up to you to know whether or not he's lying. If you go around being this gullible, this will happen. I'm not speaking to you as a man who wants to battle, I'm talking to you as your brother, Paul.

"You can break my arms and legs, break every bone in my body. I am your brother and whatever satisfies you I will do because no matter what, you're never wrong in my book. You don't understand brother, life will be difficult being alone. I was alone without you nor Sean for four years, yet you were alone even longer," he persuaded as Byron closed his eyes.

"You were five, Sean was eight, I was eleven. We lived in an orphanage after we were found sleeping in a dumpster, I remember because I was the one taking care of you guys. We used to live homeless with our parents until one day, I woke up and they were gone. There was no note, no anything. They're faces are hard to remember, but I do remember going nights on end without eating," Byron remembered as he stared at the ceiling.

"I remember bits, but not so much. Is that what really happened?" Paul asked.

"Yeah," Byron shamefully looked away from Paul. "I thought that maybe he'd come back, our father. I thought that maybe he left to get something, but we moved so it was hard to find us," he painfully uttered as a tear fell from his eyes.

"It's okay brother, we are older and smarter. We aren't weak anymore," Paul assured as collapsed to the right of Byron. "If you want to kill me, go ahead. My leg is broken and so is my arm, probably. There's been this lurking thought of human meat in my head, but I can fight those demons off," he panted as his voice faded.

"Nah," Byron thought during a moment of silence.

"I think you broke my hypnotism somehow, but I still have the powers. Awesome," Byron congratulated Paul as he squeezed his hand open and close.

"What is it anyway?" Paul wondered in an exhausted tone, his lungs burned from the air and injuries.

"I don't know, he told me that it's a condensed form of inner energy known as spirit condensing. Basically, you condense a portion of your soul energy into your hand that sends out a blast that could blow up planets," Byron explained.

"That sounds like ki condensing," Paul challenged faintly.

"They're basically the same thing. Wait, how do you know about ki condensing?" Byron asked, puzzled.

"I study books of unnatural things, I also study logical items such as mathematics books, english books, etcetera etcetera. I am a nerd in the lesser sense. I even know about life issues and stuff like that," Paul sleepily mumbled as he dozed off to dreamland.

"You are one tough man, brother."

Byron stood to his feet, brushing off the dirt from his jeans. He looked at the blood on the floor, shaking his head in disbelief. He stood over Paul, staring at him for a moment before kneeling down. He placed a hand behind his hip and one behind his shoulders, picking him up with a heave as he turned around to look for an exit.

"So, does anybody else know how to get out of a room with no windows or doors?" Gwen questioned as they stood around the throne chair.

"Well, we could always break a wall. Don't you have that one power attack you used earlier?" Bull asked Gwen.

"You were supposed to be asleep," she responded with a menacing glance. "I can't use it but once, it would exhaust me. I only exhaust myself for Paul, or Bison. Wait," Gwen stopped and began to ponder on her thoughts. "Is it wrong to like two souls yet one man?"

"Hm, if I use my powers, then we may be able to. Then again, I am not supposed to help but only give advice and tips. Would you like a tip?" The Priestess asked.

"Sure, give us a tip," Bull answered hopefully.

"You could always break a wall and see where it leads," she responded with a smile.

Bull gave her a dumbfounded stare as he said, "You're like the crappiest video game instructor."

"I mean, this is your job. I'm just giving you information to feed your little brains," she responded as he tapped her head with her finger.

A noise interrupted the silence throughout the room as if nails were being scrapped against a chalkboard. It was so loud that it made them grip their ears and fall to their knees.

"This is piercing," Bull screamed as his ears began to leak blood.

"Screw this!" Gwen yelled as she pulled out her staff and blew a condensed spirit blast into the wall to the right of the throne.

The wall broke apart outwards, sending bricks flying towards the ocean below with a splash.

"We've gotta get to Bison," Gwen instructed as she grabbed their arms and struggled to get to the opening.

Her ears bled and her heart raced as the sound got louder and faster. Each scrape was as if their own eardrum were getting scratched with a sharp knife. She fell to her knee just in front of the opening. She looked down into the ocean below, not knowing whether they were unconscious or not.

"Hey, can you guys swim?" She asked as she shook the two.

They gave a nod with their pressurized heads as Gwen tossed them both, sending them plummeting to the ocean below with a splash. Suddenly, the sounds stopped, causing Gwen to hesitate before jumping herself.

"What the?" She thought as she turned around to another hole in the wall, but across from her. "Is this an illusion?" She pondered while she turned around to see that the hole she made was covered.

"Who's there?" She regretted asking as she felt a shove from behind herself, causing her to lose balance and fall.

Manic laughter filled the room as it echoed off of the walls. Gwen turned around onto her back and began to look around the room as it began to spin, causing her to flop from side to side as the room also rotated. The laughter stopped and a raspy voice was heard from around the room as Gwen stopped getting tossed around.

"So, you are Gwen? I remember you from the underworld when I visit," the voice began as the walls disappeared into darkness, plunging Gwen into a void of darkness.

"Who are you?" Gwen asked as she stood to her feet angrily. "Tell me and I might spare you."

"There is no reason, for you cannot see me and I am not here to kill you. Do you not remember an ally when one is in your face?" It asked.

"I have no allies but Bison and his crew. What do you want?"

A projector screen appeared in front of her, the light emitted from behind her as she turned around and stared at the live camera feed. There was a man in chains, hoisted on a wall with his shirt off. There was blood dripping from his legs and face as he stared blankly at the ground.

"Who are you?" she asked as she turned around to see who was controlling the screen. Nothing but darkness surrounded her, except for a magical light.

"We may not be allies, but I do not like destroyers. I guide lost souls to the afterlife, I do not indulge in evil manners. However, your father put me in charge to guide you while you walk upon the Earth. I'm basically an ally at your aid in times like these."

"Tell my father I don't want his charity," she snapped, annoyed.

"You're prince is being held hostage not too far from here," the voice faded as the room returned to normal.

He stared at the puddle of blood underneath his feet and a drip was seen to fall from his toes. His vision blurred as the blood dripped from his hopeless eyes. A man in a hooded robe stood in front of the bars of the jail with his hands clasped together underneath his sleeves.

"How do you feel?" The man asked, his voice was raspy as if he were parched.

The prisoner weakly looked at the man in the robe, gritting his teeth as he strained his neck. Anger began to flow through his veins as he attempted to move. The chains rattled as it hung him above the floor with his chest pushed outwards.

"The future foretold of a man who could destroy omniverses, and thanks to a variety of convenient events, we might have him in our clutches. Would you like to hear a story?" The man asked as he turned around and grabbed a chair from the table sitting behind him.

He sat in front of the cage that held the man captive, whose voice was unable to perform due to his slit throat.

"There were a total of four warriors who hopped from dimension to dimension. From timeline to timeline, from universe to universe. If you hadn't gotten the picture, they hopped from omniverse to omniverse to foil the plans the Low Priest had for the lands he wanted to conquer. He caught them in a rare trap, as you've seen earlier, in the apocalypse that can mask his evil aura. The planet he stands on will not explode because of his, how do I say, container energy.

"It's basically when you can eject your aura onto the Earth's atmosphere, catching and absorbing any energy that tries to escape. The Earth is protected due to the neutralization it has on the Earth's crust, it's barely affected. He could eject his aura around a galaxy, solar system, universe, omniverse, it doesn't matter. If the High Priest, however, were to descend upon Earth as himself, the entire solar system would explode.

"I'm pretty sure you know that when two beings of high power fight it could cause a collapse in all of the omniverses, causing a wake in the verse outside of the omniverse. There is a long, long, long space between the edge of the omniverses and the edge of the demiverses where at one high end lives the High Priest. The lower space is inhabited by the Low Priest, which if it were up to him, the all of the omni-verses would be his to control instead of the High Priest.

"Back to the warriors, whenever there was a distress call from any omni-verses' universe, they were sent down to settle the score. Multiple Earths are attacked at the same time everyday, so how do you ensure the safety of every earth in the same span? That's easy, you just adjust the time everything happens. See, the High Priest is a demi-verse demon meant to watch over the omni-verses. He recruited four people to defend territory on his behalf.

"Though being quite the show off, he is more powerful than his younger brother, the Low Priest. Growing up, they battled in unbreakable voids and shattered every dimension that they were in contact with," the man concluded as he looked at Bison.

His eyes weakly adjusted to the man's face, groaning from trying to speak. Blood leaked from his neck like a leaking faucet, and every connection to joints was cut off. A man in a white robe, Byron, walked into the room and began to talk to the man.

"Has he regenerated anything?" Byron asked the man he stood next to him and stared at Bison.

"Not yet, we've only been here twenty minutes. You've gotta give it time," the man argued.

"Time is not of the essence, our Lord does not like to wait," Byron urged.

"True, but he will understand. Now that we have him, we can start our mission to kill the High Priest."

"We already have," Byron reassured as he exited the room.

"So, does anyone know what to do about revived aqua life?" Bull questioned in a panic as he floated in the sea.

He looked to the hole in the tower to see Gwen spear dive into the sea, nearly hitting the rocks as she splashed. The High Priestess floated in a bubble and watched the two swim frantically around to find land. She turned around to see what seemed to be a gigantic shark fin advancing towards their location.

"Heads up guys," she warned after a whistle, causing the two to look in the direction of the disturbed waters.

"Wait, wait, I can't swim that good," Bull panicked as he flopped around helplessly.

Suddenly, something yanked Gwen underwater, gripping her boot as the water split apart beneath her. She gasped for air mere milliseconds before entering the depths of the blue. She stared down at her foot, attempting to make a visual on her attacker. She let her arms free fall upwards as she used all of her force to try and pry her foot free.

Noticing how useless it was, she began to wait until they've gotten to their destination. Gwen was able to hold her breath for up to an hour underwater and in space due to training in the underworld. She felt gravity pull her down to the bottom of an underwater cave clearing as the hand released her foot. She banged her head as she collapsed onto the ground, causing her to lose consciousness.

Chapter 13

Bulls redemption

"Where'd she go?" Bull asked as he flayed around, attempting to keep his head above water.

"You really are useless, aren't you?" The Priestess taunted as she floated above him.

"You're the one just sitting there, I'm actually in the ocean," he contested as the shark fin got closer.

"I'm only here to enact on three objectives. One is to teach and inform you all on the current and future situations. My second is to take you to your trainer. My last is to train you in realistic situations such as this one. Survive this and we'll have good news to tell the High Priest, or do you not fear death?" She asked as she looked at the towering shark fin within just mere feet of Bull.

He stared at the fin that was now in front of him, nearly running into him as it passed him. He saw now that it wasn't a regular shark, it was a megalodon. His thoughts began to jumble into a ball as panic settled and the waves threw him around the sea of fields.

"Gwen just got pulled under and all you can do is panic when an enemy is near. Are you letting your human side take over, or are you just a natural coward. I once saw potential in you, but now all I see is failure," the High Priestess taunted in disappointment as she turned her back towards Bull.

As the megalodon swam past for a second time, this time with ill intention, Bull grabbed the fin as it attempted to hit him with its huge jaw. He hung onto the fin as it shook him around like a cowboy on a bull. It dove underwater, sending Bull under the human death trap of water. His breath was minimal due to him using so much energy to ride the shark, and his lungs burned.

He held his breath for what seemed to be an eternity as the megalodon tried to shake the object on its tail. It spun in circles and swam football fields before Bull passed out, letting go of the megalodon and floating deeper under the depths. Water filled his lungs as he stared at the surface tension, reliving his past as it displayed like a movie in front of him.

"Who am I really?" Bull began to question himself as he thought. "I just wanted to live the American dream, where I have a happy family and I have to work everyday. Go home to my wife and kid. But if it ever came down to it, could I protect them if I tried? Maybe that's why The Creator took them away from me, to teach me a lesson. But, in the end, I failed due to my cowardness," he concluded as he floated downwards, staring at the huge fish that was about to engulf him.

The waters split apart as gravity pulled Bull to the bottom of the sea. The shark was pushed aside with all of the water as if it were something to just split in half. Bull looked up in a haze as his vision blurred and lungs burned to see the High Priestess sitting in her bubble above the waters.

"I have heard your thoughts my child," she began as what seemed like her staff was pointed in Bulls direction. "You will learn to not be afraid of yourself and those around you. Having a family is good, but when a higher calling is knocking at your door and you ignore it, the family will suffer. Those things you hold dear to your heart are the things that need to motivate you. Take that anger from your dead family and use it to your advantage. Find her killers and exact your revenge. You are Bull, and nothing will stand in your way. Bison would have a problem defeating you even with his high spirit energy," she gloated as her staff began to glow.

"All of my children can neutralize each other out, there are no favorites here. Yeah one may be stronger than the other, but the one can counter the stronger one and make him fail."

A light illuminated from the staff, sending a bubble to the nearly unconscious Bull. It entrapped him, holding him still as it lifted him towards the Priestess.

"Let's get your brother back, and Gwen I guess," she said to herself as she flew out into space. They left everything to rot on the Earth as demons and zombies fought in boredom.

Her head ached as she sat up with one hand on the ground and the other on her head. She looked around with squinting eyes, attempting to make out images of what seemed to be dungeon walls.

"Is this where Paul is?" She asked herself as she realized her mask was gone. "Well, now they're going to pay, but first I need to get out of here."

She began to walk around the room as her vision began to clear and she inspected the room. There were both old and fresh blood stains sprayed everywhere, even on the ceiling. The cell was only big enough that it could only fit possibly two people, and the bars were not of metal but were of an infusion of spirit energy and steel. Gwen yanked at the bars testing their endurance and to her surprise, they were heavily durable. There was no bed or window as she turned around to inspect the area a little bit more, looking for an object to use.

She concluded it was useless for there was nothing around, not even a rock.

Where was she? This wasn't just some underground cell underneath an Earth. These were thoughts that bothered Gwen as she paced the room with her arms folded to her chest. She stared at the ground with anger as the walls began to darken and the hallway she was held in plummeted into a pure darkness. Guards began to panic as they wandered the hallway hopelessly, running into walls and crashing into each one other. They began to choke as if there were something stuck in their throat, collapsing to the ground with multiple thuds.

The room to the end of the hallway opened, causing her darkness to spill into the newly discovered room.

"What's going on in here?" The guard barked as he swung the door open.

He stopped walking as soon as he noticed the darkness, it was hard to tell exactly where he was.

"What the hell?" He asked as he stood baffled in front of the door, fear gripped his mind as he stood in shock. All the man could see when he opened the door was a wall of darkness.

The man behind him abruptly awoke from his sleep, causing the magazine that rested on his face to fall to the ground. His chair fell backwards as his legs were propped onto the table, causing him to collapse onto his back. He fell to his right side, placing his hands on the ground as his feet were thrown to the floor. He stood to his feet and stared into the dark abyss with amazement and fear.

"What is this?" He asked his partner as he looked to the ground.

He yelped as he looked to the ground to see that the darkness wasn't only in the hallway, it was now in their room. It suddenly erupted, sending a spike of darkness into the man's face that encumbered the entire room into pitch black nothingness.

"Sir," a guard busted into the office Byron occupied. "An entire sector of the jail has been encumbered by darkness. We closed the doors leading to anything further, that seems to have stopped the darkness's movement."

"What?" Byron shouted as he slammed his hands onto the table, abruptly standing up in anger.

A guard sat behind him on a metal chair next to three lockers.

"Which sector?" He asked as he looked to his left at the lockers.

"Sector H, the one that held Bison's guardian," he responded.

"That's not too far from Bison's sector, get me a report from Viper," he commanded as he opened the lockers.

A large blade rested onto the back of the locker where a barely visible handle was seen. He picked it up, holding it at an arm's length away from himself. Byron swung it from his left to his right with great swiftness, causing the entire entrance of the room and the hallway to be cut in half.

"Sir," the same guard from earlier entered Bison's holding sector as the man, Viper, was still rambling nonsense to Bison.

He stopped talking and looked at the guard with an unimpressed expression as he walked closer.

"Come closer and you die, understand servant?" He warned without flinching.

The man stopped walking, clasping his arms and legs to his sides as his body tensed.

"There's been a breach in sector H, Byron wants to know if there are any updates for him," he asked nervously as sweat poured from his face and his lips quivered in fear.

"Not yet, are we under attack?" Viper asked as he stood to his feet, turning his attention onto Bison.

"No sir, do you not know we captured Gwen?" He responded.

"What?" Viper yelled in shock as he snapped his attention to the guard. "How?"

"There were some sea mermaids the Low Priest hired to drag her underwater to a cave and let gravity drop her head onto the ground. It worked pretty well since they were pretty fast swimmers, they then teleported here."

"No no no no no," Viper repeatedly uttered as he whipped his attention back to Bison to see him standing to his feet as blood still dripped from his neck, staring at the ground.

The gashes that once disabled his armpit, arms, legs, and feet were covered by fresh skin. The room began to shake as the two began tumbling onto their asses, staring at the caged animal. Viper stared in amazement as the guard stared in horror and wind began to freely rush throughout the room, making them float.

Viper swiped his hand out in front of him, sending a stronger wind to negate the current wind. Sending the entire room into a hurricane, the walls began to break as the wind grew stronger and stronger by the millisecond.

"As long as he's in the cage, there's nothing he can do!" Viper yelled in excitement.

The guard was seen to be getting tossed around like a ragdoll, smashing into the walls as the paint began to peel apart.

"He might actually attempt to tear the walls down," he yelled in concern. "No matter, these walls don't lead to the outside like on Earth, it'll lead to the outer space we're surrounded in."

Suddenly the wind calmed down, causing the objects to finish their flight as they scattered around the floor. Viper fell onto his back, staring at Bison who stared into his soul. Fear gripped his throat as he attempted to talk, the sight of Bison scared the life out of him.

"Where is she?" Bison asked as the skin that parted his neck began to close.

"I had no idea Bison, we're sorry," Viper began pleading as he cautiously stood to his feet. His hands were in front of him as if to ward him off with a shove.

"I do not care for my own life," Bison began with calm anger in his voice "The only reason I fight is to protect my family and those who are innocent. Men like you, taking protectors away from the weak, it angers me deeply," he scoffed as he abruptly grabbed the steel bars.

"You protagonist killers, the ones who want to conquer and kill for their own selfish desires. For those that want to kill innocents for their own profit, for those who call themselves heroes, yet put civilians into harm's way. I'll defeat you all, even those who claim their seats in heavens above the Earth, for these powers you hold were given to you from The Creator himself," Bison rambled as he pulled the two bars away from each other.

"You know about mythological gods and goddesses too?" Viper asked in amazement.

The door to the sector opened as an obviously mad Byron entered the room. His sword was in hand as he approached Viper.

"I'm killing him here and now," he mumbled as he stomped to the open cell door.

He held his sword out in front of the unfazed Bison as Bison stared into Byron's eyes with anger and pain. Viper stood beside Byron not too far away.

"You know we can't kill him," Viper warned Byron as they stood silent.

"I know I'm stronger," he snarked with solemn confidence.

"We can test that, my energy is one hundred percent and Paul is nowhere to be seen." Bison taunted as he stood there, his all black eyes still stared into Byron's eyes.

They stood in complete silence as it seemed that minutes passed while they waited for each other to throw the first strike.

"Give me a reason to not kill him," Byron directed his words towards Viper.

"Ask me, I'm your brother," Bison taunted as he took a step forward, causing the blade to press against his nose.

Byron steadied his stance with his left foot rested in front of him while the right stood sturdy against the ground.

"You and I haven't been trained in that area yet,"

"Shut it, the Priest transferred everything I needed to my brain. I'm stronger than Viper there," he bragged, nodding towards Viper.

The door to the cell room began to open, making everyone's head turn towards the motion. A guard entered the room looking rather small for a man.

"The Priest wants an update on the current situation, whats going on?" He asked, his hat curiously layed low over his face as he asked.

"No prison guards have contact with the Priest, only me and Viper do. Who are you?" Byron asked as he lowered his sword and walked towards the guard, shoving Viper to the side.

"Just someone sent from HQ, I was given this uniform to blend in." He responded nervously.

"If you're from HQ, what's your badge number?" Byron asked with a smirk.

They stood in silence for a few moments as the men stood in a thick tension. Bison left his prison cell and stood behind Viper, helping him to his feet.

"Who are you?" Bison asked as he helped heave the man to his feet.

"The names Viper," he responded as he brushed himself off.

"So are you one of the Priest's servants?"

"I wouldn't entirely say that," he mumbled.

They looked at Byron and the guard to see ooze leaking from the man's boot. He stood there with his fingers on his hat and a smirk on his face before the room and the hallway that led out was encumbered into darkness.

"You doing okay down there?" The Priestess asked as she dragged Bull in a bubble beneath her.

"Yeah, but why did you save me if I was worthless?" He asked as he awoke from his sleep.

He stared into the darkness in front of him, seeing no stars but asteroids and planets in a line to meet the sun.

"You should be asking why you're so huge. You look like a brute on steroids," she bantered as she giggled.

"You're right," he blurted as he began to inspect himself. His arms and legs were bulging with unnoticeable veins, and his chest was propped outwards like he was holding his breath. His twelve pack glistened in his eyes.

"We're currently going to attempt to save your crew and retreat. We cannot fight the Low Priest at any cost," she lectured with confidence in her voice. "Even though you all have your natural talents, we're still fighting outside of the omniverses. Which means we won't be in a universe or a multiverse.

"Heck, we're not even going to be in the omniverse. We're traveling to the space between two omni-verses, which means his power is practically unlimited."

"So what's the Low Priests actual battle strategy?" Bull asked.

"We believe it's the mind, taking control and using anything he wants. From spirit energy to life energy, he can get the power just from wanting it. Mana would appear in his veins when we fought last, which was before the existence of these omni-verses."

"Wait, are you saying that there are omni-verses you guys do not see?" Bull asked obviously confused.

"I'm surprised you asked that question and not the obvious one, but yes. Since The Creator is always creating, there are portions of creation we have yet to experience. We can only see about twelve trillion omni-verses down and across. In order to do that, we have to be atop of every omni-verse, looking down on it like a God."

"Are you also saying you're not Gods?"

"Exactly. Me and my husband like to look at ourselves as if we were some watcher of creation. We did not create creation, The Creator did."

"You're mighty humble," he mumbled, turning around to look behind himself.

"We have to be, if we weren't humble then the omni-verses wouldn't have peace. Let's say we decide to destroy an omni-verse or a universe based on evil deeds done in said universe. We would not because we are not in the position to judge. We only seek to help and to not destroy, unlike the Low Priest. All he wants is destruction."

"Why?" Bull asked as a solar system was seen to be getting smaller as they flew away from it.

"He thinks that since The Creator keeps creating, there's no purpose in letting it rest. There should be judgements and punishment along with human sins, he believes."

"What's going to happen to Gwen and Bison," he asked as he sat hopelessly waiting.

"They're probably going to get experimented on, if they didn't escape their jail cells. I'm guessing that Paul is dead and they couldn't do anything to Gwen since, well, she's Gwen."

"So what does that mean?" He asked with a heavy bass in his voice.

"It means that the Low Priest will make an appearance if his servants cannot control them.

"So where are we now?"

"We're traveling over stray solar systems in the dimensions. Basically, we're in the space between the universe we left and the universe we're going to be going directly down from," she tried explaining.

"Why are we going downwards?"

"To get to base Viper just outside of the omni-verse you once called home. There are truly strong enemies there, even the guards could be dangerous to regular humans."

"Is that where Byron is stationed?"

"Yes, and the actual owner of base Viper is Viper himself. I've never seen his face before even though we can see everything. It's like he's wearing a cloaking device specifically designed to negate us," she explained as they approached their neighboring universe.

"So does that mean it's a possibility that Bison and Gwen could be in danger?"

"It's not a possibility, it's definite. Without proper training, the only person's natural talent that can be used is yours. You are the damage mitigator that will ensure the survival of his team. You're a natural born leader, you've just gotta trust yourself," she finished as they slowed to a stop.

"Why are we stopping?" He asked as he looked around the dark void of space to only see the universe they hovered over.

"This is where we drop," she informed as they plummeted downwards at an unbelievable speed.

"I'm coming for you Viper, whoever you are," she thought to herself.

The darkness began to fade as the colors leaked back to life, revealing Viper and Byron to be hanging from the ceiling like spider food.

"Did you have to hang them like that?" Bison asked Gwen as she returned to her normal body.

"One's your brother and if I killed the other one, it would disturb natural order," she explained, giving a death glare to Viper.

They walked out of Bisons holding cell room and began to walk towards the right, hoping to run into an exit.

"Where do you think we are?" Gwen asked as she looked around the narrow hallway.

The hallway was small and slim, with little to no room to stretch out, it could only hold two people at a time.

"We're probably in outer space. By the way the hallways and rooms are built, it's a spaceship that's the letter V. Honestly when the guard said sector H, it kind of threw me off because in my earlier interrogation, the Low Priest was talking about having only three sectors. Two at the top and one at the bottom," Bison explained as he stared lifelessly at the ground.

"Hey, what's wrong Bison?" she asked in a panic as she watched his body slump lifelessly against the wall.

His voice was weak and his skin was pale as he slid down the wall.

"This is and isn't my body," Bison explained. "The original host had all control, and since I am technically Paul's son, I cannot control this body. In my prediction, I was created from his spirit but a spirit needs to have an original host to live in the mortal world. Me, I never hosted a body, so I technically never existed in this world," he tried explaining as he could barely be heard.

"You're not dying Bison, you're an immortal aren't you?" She asked as she propped him upwards, causing him to sit with his back against the wall.

"The soul is immortal, and since I only act as a stand-in for Paul when he doesn't want to fight, it means that I cannot keep control of a body I wasn't born with. All in all," he stopped talking as he fell asleep.

"Without Paul, there is no Bison," she concluded as she hoisted Bison onto her shoulder.

She began to walk down the narrow hallway in quick haste, attempting to not run into enemies. Gwen ran for what seemed an eternity down this narrow hallway, slowing her speed as she saw a man with his back turned towards her.

She stopped jogging and began to slowly walk towards the man in dark crimson red. He stood in front of a yellow door with an exit sign above it.

"So, you're Gwen?" the man asked in a deep trembling voice. "I remember your mother," he taunted as he turned around.

Gwen gritted her teeth and balled up her fists in anger as her aura began to project outwards. It quickly sped towards the man not too far in front of her at high speeds, targeting his feet. He put a hand outward, projecting an invisible wall that stopped the darkness at the wall.

"Give me Bison and I'll let you go," he bargained, trying to tempt her.

"Never, why do you want him anyway?" Gwen asked, immediately feeling dumb for asking.

"There are deals I made with the devil, your father. Why do you fight against him instead of for him?"

"That stewardess is not my father, he's Satin, the brother of many souls that once walked the Earth." She argued as she turned her body to where Bison was far away from the Low Priest.

"How can you call him the brother of many souls?" He asked as he began to walk nonchalantly towards her. "He betrayed The Creator, so that means you're saying that all men are supposed to do evil, right?"

She backed away to give herself space from the Low Priest, keeping her hand on Bison at all costs.

"He was once an angel before becoming a devil. The world's worst devil is one that's been an angel," she snapped at him with persistence in her eyes.

"I don't want to hurt him, Gwen," he cautiously assured her as he kept his pace towards Gwen.

"If you touch him, I'll have no other choice but to kill you. Do you want to see what would happen to time and space?" She threatened.

From behind the Low Priest, she saw the door burst open as a gigantic brute was seen running at full speed. He flattened the Low Priest under his feet as he ran him over. The Priestess walked from behind the door, showing a shy smile as she began to talk.

"It's been a hell of a trip," she chuckled nervously. "Is Paul okay?"

"Paul is dead but Bison is somehow clinging onto his body," she tried explaining in simpler terms.

With the Low Priest still under one of Bulls foot, he grew angry, irritated, and frustrated as they talked.

"Well since we predict that Bison is a soul made from Paul, which means there's a bit of Paul in Bison. That must be what he's clinging to, for dear life at that," The Priestess hypothesized as she walked towards Gwen.

"I'll kill you all for putting your dirty foot on me, this is inconceivable," the Low Priest began to grumble louder and louder.

"We should leave, now!" The Priestess warned as Bull began to float.

"I'm not doing that," Bull gawked as he looked down to see the Low Priest doing a push-up with his heavy foot on him.

"What about Byron?" Gwen asked as the Priestess readied her staff, pointing it upwards.

"He chose his side, now he has to deal with the consequences. I'm here to teach lessons, not babysit," the Priestess lectured as her staff began to glow, forming bubbles around the technically three. She lifted them from the ground as she saw a glow from under Bulls bubble.

The Low Priest saw his chance fleeting as they rose to the ceiling with anger surging through his body as his aura began to project a blinding red glow. The entire base erupted in a combustion of spirit energy. The guards, the Low Priest, Viper, and Byron were still inside as he realized that his true issue was not Bison.

"Impossible that he could be protected so professionally," The Low Priest mumbled as he began to cackle in the middle of space. The sound of his laughter was heard even through the natural vacuum of space.

They turned around to look at the explosion as they flew away in their bubbles. They watched as the base popped from every portion with fire erupting from the walls in its V shape.

"He was right, the base was a V shape," Gwen mumbled as she laid Bison next to her, his breathing still faint.

"That was easier than expected," The Priestess chippered.

The three warriors began their journey back to their own omni-verse in an attempt to save anything they once loved and cherished. Will they succeed?

Printed in Great Britain
by Amazon

27346181R00110